Sun Stories

Sun Stories

Tales from Around the World

to Illuminate the Days and Nights of Our Lives

CAROLYN MCVICKAR EDWARDS

HarperSanFrancisco
A Division of HarperCollins*Publishers*

ALSO BY CAROLYN MCVICKAR EDWARDS

The Storyteller's Goddess

Permission to use the story "Raven and the Coming of Daylight" (called "Seagull's Box" in this collection) from *Coyote the Trickster: Legends of the North American Indians* by Gail Robinson and Douglas Hill, originally published by Crane & Russack, New York, 1975, granted by licensing agent Watson, Little Ltd., London.

SUN STORIES: *Tales from Around the World to Illuminate the Days and Nights of Our Lives.* Copyright © 1995 by Carolyn McVickar Edwards. All rights reserved. Printed in the United States of America. No part of this book may be used or reproduced in any manner whatsoever without written permission except in the case of brief quotations embodied in critical articles and reviews. Live storytelling of these stories is expressly encouraged, however, provided that the book is credited. For information address HarperCollins Publishers, 10 East 53rd Street, New York, NY 10022.

HarperCollins®, 📖®, and HarperSanFrancisco™
are trademarks of HarperCollins Publishers Inc.

FIRST EDITION

Illustrations by Kathleen Edwards

Library of Congress Cataloging-in-Publication Data:
Edwards, Carolyn McVickar.
Sun stories : tales from around the world to illuminate the
days and nights of our lives / Carolyn McVickar Edwards.
p. cm.
Includes bibliographical references and index.
ISBN 0–06–250276–X (pbk.)
1. Sun—Folklore. 2. Sun—Mythology. I. Title.
GR625.E38 1995   95–5858
398.26–dc20   CIP

95 96 97 98 99 ❖ RRD/H 10 9 8 7 6 5 4 3 2 1

for Lanore

The sun, I tell you, is alive, and more alive than I am, or a tree is. It may have blazing gas, as I have hair and a tree has leaves. But I tell you, it is the Holy Ghost in full raiment, shaking and walking, and alive as a tiger is, only more so, in the sky.

D. H. LAWRENCE

Contents

xi   Acknowledgments

1   Introduction

5   *Mother Sun and Her People*
CHEROKEE, NORTH AMERICA
In this epic myth, Mother Sun is transformed from petty
tyrant to compassionate life-giver.

13   *How Shapash the Sun Rescued the Prince of Fertility*
ANCIENT CANAAN
One of the oldest stories in the world, this is the Ugaritic
myth of the battle between the lord of death and the lord of
life.

24   *Spider Grandmother Finds Light for Her People*
KIOWA, NORTH AMERICA
The old arachnid's savvy and persistence is the key to bring-
ing light to a dark world.

29   *Harambee: The Story of the Pull-Together Morning*
SUKUMA, TANZANIA
In a tale for Kwanza, Mouse, Spider, and Fly cooperate to
outwit the conniving King of the Sky People.

36   *Baubo's Dance*
ANCIENT GREECE
In this seldom-told portion of the myth of Demeter and Per-
sephone, an old woman dances erotically and reawakens
Helios the Sun.

43   *Web of Fear: The Story of Akewa the Sun and Jaguar Man*
TOBA, ARGENTINA
In this ancient tale of gender politics, Akewa the Sun watches
with dismay as her fiery sisters are tricked by jaguar men into
coming down to earth forever.

51 *Surya the Sun's Marriage to Bright and Shadow*
HINDU, INDIA
This tale of Bright Image and her sister, Shadow, recounts not
only the birth of Sun but the origins of menstruation, the
major solstice of girlhood.

61 *The Rope from Heaven*
LUHYA, KENYA
A mortal woman runs away from home and comes to her ma-
turity through her relationship to Sun.

66 *How the Sun Came to Belong to Every Village*
SNOHOMISH, NORTH AMERICA
The son of the chief and his spirit-guide make a journey that
changes forever the path of the sun.

73 *How the Cock Got His Crown*
MIAO-TZU, TRIBAL CHINA
A perceptive archer proves "as above, so below" when he rids
the sky of too many suns.

78 *Sonwari and the Golden Earring*
THORIA, TRIBAL INDIA
A young bride and her father-in-law make sense of the theft
of her dowry gift by a bird of prey.

83 *The Sun Cow and the Thief*
KUTTIA KOND, TRIBAL INDIA
An outsider, haunted by happiness closed to him, steals the
light.

87 *How Marsh Wren Shot Out the Sun*
MIWOK, NORTH AMERICA
Because a spurned member of the community takes his re-
venge, Coyote and Hummingbird must save the day.

92   *The Marriage of Sun King and Silver Moon*
     THAILAND
     The stars extract a promise from a love-struck Sun.

98   *The Light Keeper's Box*
     WARAO, VENEZUELA
     Dreams, in this story, are the only strings attached to the gift
     of light.

103 *Sun Man and Grandfather Mantis*
     SAN, KALAHARI DESERT
     Honey-loving Grandfather Mantis waits for the wind to pluck
     his thinking strings to solve the dilemma of the dark.

108 *The Sun, the Stars, the Tower, and the Hammer*
     BALTS, ANCIENT NORTHERN EUROPE
     The constellations aid the Heavenly Smith in forming the
     hammer that will free Saule the Sun from her tower.

115 *Solntse, the Girl at the End of the World*
     SLAVS, ANCIENT CENTRAL AND EASTERN EUROPE
     A weary traveler finds splendor and sleep in the house of Sun.

120 *The Chanukah Story*
     JEWISH HISTORY AND LEGEND
     A guerrilla-style war against the Syrian dictator ends in the re-
     newal of the temple and a miraculous prolongation of the
     burning of the oil in the sacred lamp.

128 *The Christmas Story*
     CHRISTIAN HISTORY AND LEGEND
     Angels encourage the union of a doubt-filled couple.

134   *The Story of La Befana*
      ITALY
      An old woman named "Epiphany" flies every year to the
      houses of all the children, leaving gifts for everyone, in case
      one of them might be the king or the queen of light.

139   *Raven and the Theft of Light*
      INUIT, NORTH AMERICA
      Raven, the bird-man trickster, takes the form of a squalling
      baby to bag the moon and the sun for the people on the other
      side of the sky.

148   *Seagull's Box*
      HAIDA, NORTH AMERICA
      Gull's rigidity makes him a perfect mark for trickster Raven.

152   *Maui Snares the Sun*
      POLYNESIA
      The misshapen trickster of pan-Oceanic fame traps Sun with
      the help of his blind grandmother, who makes Sun's breakfast
      every morning.

160   *Fifth Sun*
      TOLTEC, ANCIENT MEXICO
      The deities watch Four Worlds come and go before Quetzal-
      coatl, the bird-snake-water god, sacrifices himself as the
      Scabby One for the sustenance of Fifth World.

169   *Ra and Hathor*
      ANCIENT EGYPT
      When Hathor, the Sun's Eye, takes Ra away to the dark land
      of Nubia, Anhur, the trickster, must lead them home.

181   Appendix: Mother Sun and Her People: A Play

191   Bibliography

201   Story and Motif Index

Acknowledgments

As if to teach the sun to shower out its light again, we shower one another with gifts at solstice time. These stories are my gifts to you, reader. In turn, I have been gifted by the idea of you as I have scribbled, deleted, and "saved."

Wonderful people in my everyday life have given me their love and their savvy. Mary Hurley first suggested that I collect and write sun stories. The feedback of Celia Correa, Susan Ford, and Mary Ellen Hill, three storytellers with whom I meet once a month, has been invaluable. Linda Clare and Erin Donahue found in the drafts of the stories nuance and need for development to which I was blind. Mary Jane Whitty brought "The Sun Cow and the Thief" to life. Terry Ebinger's comments deepened the "Web of Fear." Serena Herr's remarks improved the play "Mother Sun and Her People." Vi Hilbert, an Upper Skagit Elder and a relative of Chief William Shelton, talked with me about "How the Sun Came to Belong to Every Village." Brandt Creuscher of the Department of Animal Sciences at the University of California at Davis enlightened me about cows as a metaphor for the sun.

I appreciate the cheerful support of my parents, Alan and Madeleine Edwards, and I don't know what I've ever done without the dictionary they gave me. My sister, Kathleen Edwards, and Patricia Riley listened knowingly to my complaints and fears as I floundered in the too-deep water that trying to write a book so often seems. My grandmother, Helen Edwards, Sonja Ebel, and Scott Parker turned voices of respect and encouragement my way. The discussion I had with Stephanie Brown and Matthew Wadlund about solar energy issues grounded my intuitions. Glenn Turner, proprietor of Ancient Ways in Oakland, discussed with me solstice customs and introduced me to Janet McCrickard's passionate book *Eclipse of the Sun: An Investigation into Sun and Moon Myths*. My editor, Barbara Moulton, first believed in this project, and my second editor, Lisa Bach, most tactfully suggested that I try sitting in an easy chair instead of standing on a soapbox. The comments of Jeff Campbell, my copyeditor, were informed and thoughtful and definitely improved the text.

My housemate, Alaine Perry, graciously put up with my exhibitions of tension and exhaustion, calmly arranged to support my need for time and space, and asked excellently clarifying questions of my lines of thinking. Dan Mitchell imaginatively accepted the writing of this book as part of the package of being my partner.

I am indebted to Clara Sneed, whose comments about my drafts were extraordinarily helpful. She went even further and, mentorlike, helped me to imagine the parameters of my struggle to find my writing "voice."

I thank all of you from the bottom of my heart.

Sun Stories

Introduction

THE REVEREND CLEMENT MOORE wrote "A Visit from St. Nicholas" (commonly known as "The Night Before Christmas") in the nineteenth century. So powerfully did that poem's cold and dark distill a wintertime mood that even twentieth-century Southern Californians ice their suburban houses with fake snow. As a little girl in Los Angeles on Christmas Eve, I would lie in my bed hugging to myself a dream of bounty as I listened for the possible skidding of sleigh runners on the roof. Perhaps, if I just could stay awake, I might be able to hear Santa Claus stuff himself and his burden down our nonexistent chimney. I had no idea, of course, that my imagination had been caught by a winter hope as old as humankind.

No seasonal holidays are more celebrated in the modern, Euro-centric world than those that honor the Northern Hemisphere's return of the light. Even in Australia, whose actual winter solstice comes in June rather than December, people with European roots make great Christmas feasts in the heat of their summer. But today, because of electric lights, central heating, and supermarkets, we have only a dim memory of the time when the return of the light actually heralded the end of a season of deprivation and fear. Today, the winter stories we most often tell ourselves are about metaphorical suns only. A tiny sun-son is born in the Christmas story; lights in a temple stay miraculously lit in the Chanukah story; La Befana, the Italian Santa Claus, searches for a special child to light the world. We read only in our science books about the centrality of Sun in our lives. Without the sun, they tell us, there would be no green plants, and thus no food, no fuel, no life.

But crouched inside each of us is a shivering ancient, clothed in skins, huddled by a low fire. The ancient remembers. Sun and its yearly wax and wane is the mainstay of our lives. The majority of the stories in this book are old winter tales about the return not of a metaphorical sun but of the real sun, which has faded for so long that our food stores are desperately low.

At the winter solstice we stand at a threshold. In Latin, *solstice* means "sun stands still." At the summer solstice, Sun stands at the threshold of its wane. But in winter, Sun stands at the threshold of the wax of the light that promises spring. Psychologically, we stand at matching thresholds. We feel the inertia of our present position and teeter on the brink of change, which stirs in us hope and hopelessness, as well as fear, grief, surrender, and an energetic dignity otherwise known as "problem solving." Over and over again in our lives, as in these stories, we are met at the threshold not by saviors but by trick-sters whose cleverness and bodily indulgences somersault us over our own edges.

Culturally, the edge of a millennia rushes toward us. Our zeit-geist whispers that the planet is alive; that spirituality is based far more in the body and the earth than we've conceived in centuries; and that to sustain ourselves, we must live more simply, more coopera-tively, and bend our energy technologies to tap directly Sun's power.

Solstice—seasonally, psychologically, and culturally—is the time of the threshold. Sun itself pauses between decrease and increase. Be-neath our celebratory efforts, we are often sad, lonely, afraid, and ex-hausted. Many of us are pioneering seasonal solstice celebrations that reframe our bodies and the earth as the houses of our spiritualities.

On the threshold of great cultural change, we are greening our politics and our traditional understandings of religion. We are collecting multicultural myths, reorganizing our sense of gender, and revamping our metaphors for color and race. We are changing the ways we tap and use energy. We are building new cultural norms—exciting, inconvenient, and frustrating work. It is the nature of the solstian transition to swing us between hope and hopelessness.

Stories are our transitional objects. Like blankets smelling of comfort, they carry us through turbulence and chaos. They picture life the way it was, the way it can be, the way it will be. This book is a collection of stories from all over the world about the return of the sun and the light. They are stories of multiple deities, enspirited objects, lively darknesses, and tricksters. Sun in these stories is often personified: a young woman in a red dress, a red man in a chariot drawn by gold and silver horses. Sun is trapped in a tower, hiding in a cave, or packing his light in a great urn as a wedding gift. Sun is a magic sight-giver shut in a box of dreams, the gift of the rooster, or the milk of a sky cow.

Each story is introduced by remarks on its theme and culture of origin. They are tales to read, tell, paint, dance, dramatize. A play for classroom use of the Cherokee "Mother Sun and Her People" can be found in the appendix. Except for "Seagull's Box," the retellings of these myths are in my own voice. I found numerous versions of some myths, such as the Polynesian "Maui Snares the Sun." I found only one version for other stories, such as the Sukuman "Harambee." Other stories, such as the Luhyan "Rope from Heaven," were sketched in two or three paragraphs in a reference book. Still other stories, such as the Orissa tales from tribal India or the ancient Baltic tale of Saule, were summarized in just two or three sentences.

The reader who reads the book straight through will find the stories strung like beads in a necklace: each offsets its neighbors. Others will fish for stories in the small summaries in the table of contents, and still others will be intrigued with the possibilities for comparing stories offered by the Story and Motif Index at the back of the book.

The stories may surprise adults. We are steeped, after all, in the mythology of the scientific sun—a hot, gaseous star 330,000 times the size of earth, pulsing away at a distance of ninety-three million miles. But part of us joins the children in a startle of recognition. Gods and goddesses, talking animals, tricky solutions, and living suns mirror truths dozing deep inside us.

The seasonal solstice is a powerful metaphor for the psychological and cultural solstices of our lives. Waiting on the threshold in the dark, alone and together, we dare to hope for spring. We know too much and not nearly enough. We have to believe it all matters, and we have an agonizing hunch it might not. These are winter tales that sew from all the scraps a quilt of hope, wisdom, and humor.

Mother Sun and Her People

FROM THE CHEROKEE NATION, NORTH AMERICA

Solstice, like all seasonal change, is actually a gradual transition. Winter sunlight returns slowly, its increase barely perceptible. Yet our sense of extremes at solstice time is acute. The solstian tableau of a tiny light born in a huge darkness is a metaphor for a hope and pleasure we feel birthing inside of fear, sadness, and hopelessness. Though we moderns blithely flip electric light switches and frequent the magical cornucopias called supermarkets, our difficult seasonal feelings are oddly strong. They are feelings rooted in an old survival drama in which, each winter, worry about the return of literal light, food supply, and the continuation of life itself shrouded the village.

Modern questions of survival no longer seem so clear-cut. Yet the seasonal solstice provokes in us a strong uneasiness and mirrors the confusion of every other psychological passage we experience. Psychological passages, in fact, function as psychological solstices. Solstices are times of transition and threshold. They require that we deal with death, change, and limits: the old position is dying, and we must cross to the new. We feel polarized, yet our emotions and options are rarely simply black and white. We tumble across a turbulent palette of physical, intellectual, emotional, and spiritual color. Ambivalence and aberration tint everything.

Today, at the edge of the millennium, we stand in the midst of an ecological and cultural solstice. Our culture must make hard choices about its use of energy. Our supplies of indirect solar energy—oil and coal—are dwindling. Nuclear technology is poisonous. The ways we now use energy deny real limits and endanger health. In order to thrive in the long run, we must accept the dying of our old ways and learn to capture solar energy directly from the sun. We know a lot about how to do that. But despite our current technological savvy, the political and personal "hows" of using solar energy directly for most of our needs are anything but clear, convenient, and easy.

Myths are the maps for our passages—whether they are seasonal, psychological, or eco-cultural. Maps picture routes and destinations at the same time. Myths, too, picture complex processes and give us images of wholeness.

This Cherokee myth can be read as a story of seasonal and psychological transition. Its subject is of epic proportions. Its style is folksy and humorous, but it comments on no less than the role of death in our lives. The characters in the myth are forced into relationship with limits and death. Mother Sun both causes and experiences death. She stands for arbitrary circumstances and for the struggle to cope. The many opposites in this story finally cluster around a center of integrative acceptance and creativity.

The myth also seems to be a story of great cultural transition. In the early nineteenth century, the lifestyle of the Cherokee Nation was extraordinarily similar to that of their European-immigrant neighbors. Unlike many other native tribes, the Cherokee were not nomadic. In fact, their settlements could hardly be distinguished from other farm towns in the state of Georgia. Some Cherokee even owned huge cotton plantations and black slaves. They published their own newspaper. Their government and court systems were nearly identical with those of the United States. They had even fought with U.S. cavalry against their Creek Indian neighbors. Nonetheless, when gold was discovered on Cherokee territory, Congress gave permission in 1838 for "Indian removal." Over a six-month period, seven thousand U.S. soldiers drove fourteen thousand Cherokee west from Georgia to Oklahoma, over what was later called the "Trail of Tears." Drought, extreme cold, measles, and whooping cough struck the marchers. One of every four Cherokee died.

The story of Mother Sun and her daughter was collected in the 1890s. Though the story may be very old, the teller of this tale was very likely alive, probably an adult at the time of the Trail of Tears. The realities of the Trail of Tears may well have shaped his emphases.

This story has motifs in common with many sun stories, as the Story and Motif Index readily shows. Sun is a woman; redbird plays a part; a box is a central prop. The dance to attract the Cherokee Mother Sun from her seclusion is like the spirit dance to attract the Japanese Mother Sun Amaterasu Omikami from her cave (see The Storyteller's Goddess, *Edwards*).

Mother Sun and Her People

Mother sun's face was red. Pacing back and forth, she gesticulated as she spoke. Moon sat listening, a little slumped, his pale lips pressed together. He looked down sadly at Earth tilting below them. Mother Sun and Moon had had this conversation before.

"Oh stop mooning," fumed Mother Sun.

"I feel sorry for them," said Moon.

"Yeah, well, you can afford to. They look at you like they love you—all soft and smiling. I'm sick of it."

"Mother Sun," said Moon. "They seem ugly to you because you don't realize how hard it is to look at you when you're like this."

"Like what? I'm just being me, and they squinch up their faces in ugly pouts every time they look at me."

"They're your grandchildren," said Moon. "If they could hear you talk like this, they'd be even more upset."

"Well, I'm tired of your sniveling and I've had it with them. They may not be able to hear me, but they're going to feel me," she added grimly.

Moon sighed. "You're a vindictive old woman," he said and faded away.

Mother Sun stalked over to her daughter's house for her usual noontime lunch.

"Mother," said Sun Daughter. "What are you doing?"

Mother Sun was standing just outside the house, arms raised high, sending down her most ferocious heat to the people below. "I'm trying to kill them," she puffed. "They're ugly and they like Moon better than me, and I'm going to punish them."

Sun Daughter watched for a while, then shook her head. "I don't know why you can't just let this go. Why do you insist that they act just like you want them to?"

Mother Sun paid no attention. She continued to pour out her heat.

Sun Daughter's red dress fluttered. "Come inside, Mother," she said finally. "I've got your favorite yellow squash soup."

Mother Sun, who was tired anyway, allowed herself to be led inside. But seated at the table, she continued to punctuate her rapid chewing with bitter remarks about Moon and the grandchildren.

Meanwhile, the people below were falling ill by the hundreds. Afraid and sorrowful, they sent a group of leaders to the Little People, who live under the world. The opening to the underworld was small but, once inside, so blessedly cool that the heat from the fires of the Little People felt comforting.

"Mother Sun is trying to kill you," the Little People explained. "You must find a way to kill her instead. We will help." In huge black cauldrons, the Little People stirred up the medicine to form four poisonous snakes.

"Send Spreading Adder and Copperhead first," they instructed. "If those two can't kill her, send the others."

Spreading Adder and Copperhead slithered to the top of the sky. Nervously, they coiled beside Sun Daughter's door. Spreading Adder flicked his tongue while Copperhead practiced his most frightening posture. But when Mother Sun strode into view, having made her journey from the other side of the sky vault, Spreading Adder cowered in her blinding light. All he could do was to spit yellow slime.

Mother Sun saw only Copperhead. "You nasty old thing," she said, and stepped over him.

Ashamed, Spreading Adder and Copperhead slunk away.

Then, during the night, Rattlesnake and Water Monster sneaked up to Sun Daughter's house. Water Monster's tail covered Moon and the stars with dark clouds. Everyone was sure Water Monster, with his terrible eyes and horns, would assassinate Mother Sun quickly and bring this plague of heat to an end.

The two reptiles lurked outside Sun Daughter's door. Rattlesnake twitched at every sound, so eager was he to be helpful.

"Would you just calm down?" said Water Monster irritably. "She doesn't get here till noon."

But Rattlesnake's jumpiness got the better of him. Just before noon, when Sun Daughter opened her door to look for her mother, Rattlesnake struck and killed her.

"Fool!" shouted Water Monster. "That was the wrong one!" In a fury, he churned back to the people below. There he complained and threatened so venomously that the people had to send him to the end of the world, where he remains to this day.

Mother Sun found her daughter's body, still warm in the doorway. Her jealousy of Moon and her plans for punishing the earth broke to pieces inside her. She gathered her child in her arms. Sun Daughter's ghost peeled away from her form and trembled over the wailing mother. Then Sun Daughter's spirit flitted away to Ghost Country in the Darkening Land in the West.

Mother Sun shut herself inside her daughter's house and refused to come out. The people were no longer dying of heat, but now they lived in total darkness.

Once more the grandchildren asked the Little People for help. "Send seven men with seven sticks and a good strong box to Ghost

Country," instructed the Little People. "Use the sticks to capture Sun Daughter in the box—and fetch her home. When Mother Sun has her child again, she will shine for you. But whatever you do, whatever she says, don't open that box till she's safe with her mother."

For seven days the seven men with seven sticks and a good strong box traveled to Ghost Country. Whirling in the circles of spirits dancing there, the seven men found Sun Daughter in her smoky red dress. Each time she passed, one of the men touched her with his stick. At the seventh touch, Sun Daughter rose up out of the Ghost Dance and the men folded her into the box. The dance of the Ghost People quickened.

Carrying the precious box, the seven men began the journey east. But before long, Sun Daughter's voice wheedled out of the box. "Please let me out!" The men looked at one another, but did not answer.

"I'm so hungry!" Sun Daughter said pitifully.

"I can't breathe in here!" she moaned. "I'm dying!"

The men felt afraid. Suppose she did die and they were not able to bring her alive to her mother? The people might send them, as they had Water Monster, to the end of the world. The men shrugged helplessly. They opened the box a tiny crack.

With a fluttering, something flew past them. A bright Redbird lit on a nearby bush. Frightened, the men opened the box all the way. Sun Daughter was gone! But in her new form of Redbird, she began to warble a song. In great dismay, the men tried to catch her. But Sun Daughter, forever Redbird now, took wing. If only the men had kept the box closed, we would always have been able to bring back the people we love from the Ghost Country. But alas, it isn't so! The men shut the lid on the empty box and forced themselves to return to the settlements.

Mother Sun screamed when she opened the box. When she'd heard of the seven men's journey, she had clung to the hope that she might be able to see her child again. Now she understood that her daughter would never come back. She wept tears that flooded the entire world.

In hopes of saving themselves from the drowning darkness, the people held council. They sent up a group of children to drum and dance for Mother Sun. Clinging to one another's hands, the youngsters danced the most winning dance they could. Mother Sun, however, seemed to pay no attention. All was dark, wet, and freezing cold.

Then, without warning, the drummers changed their beat. The dancers dropped hands, and each began a separate leaping and twirling, faster and faster. The quickened rhythm was so exciting that Mother Sun stopped crying and could not help herself from peeking. When they saw her face, the dancers rippled into a rainbow of joy.

Mother Sun's eyes filled again with tears. But this time she did not spill them. She gazed at her dancing and singing grandchildren. How alive they were! And not ugly at all. Mother Sun smiled tremulously and opened the door. Stepping outside, she, very gently, raised her arms.

How Shapash the Sun Rescued
the Prince of Fertility

FROM ANCIENT CANAAN

This myth, one of the oldest stories in the world, has the modern flavor
of an adventure comic book. It can be read as a map for both seasonal
and psychological solstices. Winter arrives, the god of green disappears;
Sun is responsible for bringing him back. The way of the psyche always
calls for balance: both the king of fertility and the king of sterility must
be given their due.

A myth can describe human experiences never dreamed of by its
originators. We moderns find ourselves in an eco-cultural transition for
which this ancient tale may bear direction. Baal, King of the World,
throws himself an extravagant party in his opulent new castle. Like so
many of us in the energy-profligate "first world," Baal fails to include
Mot, the Lord of Death, among the glitterati on his guest list. Indeed,
Mot is Lord of Entropy—that simple rule of physics so repugnant to and
little known by the most reckless users of energy on the planet. Entropy
is the law that promises ultimate death for everything, that predicts that
all energy disperses finally until it is static and irretrievable. The Law of
Entropy promises ends and final death. But Entropy neither predicts nor
controls the speed at which we advance toward those limits. The more
simply we live, the less energy we expend, the longer the time we have.

In the eco-cultural reading of this myth, it is probably no accident
that Baal's fatal excursion to the underworld is preceded by his osten-
tatious expenditures of energy. Baal finds that his way back to life is a
direct relationship with Sun, mother of all energy. The modern technology we have for a direct relationship with the sun is also "entropically
sound." Though every use of energy must finally submit to the Law of
Entropy, the use of direct solar energy will drastically slow our advance
toward that end. Solar technology obliges us to use labor- rather than

energy-intensive, small-scale processes and machinery and to lead lifestyles that focus on the simple, the reusable, and the homemade.

The discovery in 1928 of the Ras Samra Tablets on the site of the ancient city of Ugarit in north Syria opened up new understandings of this prebiblical Semitic mythology. Before this, we were aware of these myth cycles only through fragments preserved by Greek historiographers. The Ras Samra Tablets, badly damaged, are written in what looks like cuneiform, but it is actually an alphabet. The language—related to Arabic, Aramaic, and Hebrew—was unknown before the discovery of the tablets and is now called Ugaritic. The tablets date from the fourteenth century B.C.E., but their stories have much earlier origins. Their three major myths tell of the adventures of Baal and of two kings, Keret and Aqhat. An Egyptian version of this Ugaritic myth, the Astarte Papyrus, dating between 1550 and 1200 B.C.E., bridges the gaps in Baal's story that have literally been destroyed by time.

Shapash the Sun plays a central role in this story because of her unique ability to travel freely back and forth from the under- to the upperworld. Here, Baal is simply the prince of fertility, but in later stories he supplants the father god El. He eventually became identified with so many different deities—including the Hebrew Yahweh—that his name came to mean simply "lord," representing a composite of many gods. In Arabic, rain-watered soil is still called "land of Baal," while arid and barren places are called mawat, a cognate with the name of Mot, prince of sterility. The "water boy" god Ashtar, too small to be king of the earth, represents the power of artificial irrigation. Athtari in Arabic, a form of Ashtar, still refers to soil so watered. Baal's sister, the goddess Anat, rules over war and slaughter as well as love and fertility. Astarte, Baal's love interest, is queen of the night sky. The souls of humans not yet born and already dead live in her stars (see "Astarte, the Guiding Star" in The Storyteller's Goddess, Edwards).

How Shapash the Sun Rescued the Prince of Fertility

HERE IS THE STORY OF THE first time Mot, Lord of the Drought, made Baal, Prince of the Rain, a prisoner in his underworld. It happened then and it happens still. Long live Shapash the Sun, the Queen of Day, who carries him forth again and again to reign over Earth as King of Life. This is how it came to pass.

Baal, the Cloud Rider, was celebrating his victory over Yamm, the Dragon of the Sea. He had caused a new palace to be built for himself, magnificent enough for his newly won position as King of the World. For its walls, he had cut down cedars on ten thousand acres. For its adornment, seven whole mountains had yielded their silver, gold, and jewels. He stood now in its splendid dining hall. A great feast had been laid on seven hundred and seven golden tables. Before his guests arrived, he set his two magic axes on display, admiring their gleaming efficacy. Kothar, the Heavenly Smith, had made them. Driver and Repeller were their names. The gold of Driver and the silver of Repeller glinted against the translucent violet-blue of the lapis lazuli insets in the wall behind them. Baal swelled with pride.

"I have avenged the gods and goddesses of Heaven against the sea monster Yamm!" Baal proclaimed to the vaults of the ceiling, smiting his chest with both fists.

The feud of Baal the Cloud Rider and Yamm the Sea Dragon was very old. They had battled continually over which of the two, Rain God or Ocean God, would be Lord of the Earth. Finally, Father El himself, on the Mountain at the Far Horizon, wrapped in the azure cloak of the sky, had had to intervene. Baal still smarted at the memory of El's decision to allow Yamm to rule Earth.

"But I showed him!" yelled Baal to the echoing walls. "I showed El who is King!"

Indeed, as Lord of the Earth, Yamm had proved so tyrannical in his demand for tribute from the gods and goddesses that they had reinstigated Baal's old war with the Dragon of the Sea. But Father El had commanded them to stop. "Yamm is more powerful," warned El. "He will kill Baal, and I won't allow that."

Baal's obedience had been grudging. But when the apple of Baal's eye, the long-necked, heavy-haired Astarte, had succeeded in charming Yamm into inviting her to live with him under the sea in exchange for less tribute from all the other deities, Baal's rage had erupted. With the help of Driver and Repeller, Baal smote the scaly neck of the Dragon Yamm and left him for dead on the shore.

"And then Anat," Baal shook his head, thinking of his beautiful sister, "without Anat . . . "

Anat, teeth even and white as a flock of goats on the side of a dusky mountain, had seen that Yamm was not really dead. She had beaten his gluttonous coils mercilessly and kicked him back into the depths of the sea. Even now, Kothar the Heavenly Smith was fashioning a net for Yamm from which Baal was certain the Sea Dragon would never escape. So sure was Baal that he was free forever from Yamm's spying and interferences that he had even allowed Kothar to make a giant window for his palace.

Baal looked out of his new window. As the true King of the Earth now, he could easily send through this window the snow, the rain, and the moisture in all the right seasons.

Baal's tables were laden with the rarest of wines, the crispest of breads, the plumpest of quince and raisin cakes, and the most succulent of meats. By the time Baal's guests arrived, he had perfumed himself with myrrh and arrayed himself in robes of silver and white. Belted and braceleted with grape vines, he wore narcissus flowers for his crown.

Kothar the Smith, decked in sprigs of pale-blue-berried juniper, had a seat of honor on the great block of his anvil beneath Driver and Repeller, the magical weapons.

Ashtar, the Water Boy, eyes shining, shook Baal's hand. "Could I touch Driver and Repeller, my lord?" he asked reverently. Baal smiled kindly and stepped aside so the boy could get closer to the weapons.

Baal's sister, Anat, in jewelled scarlet the color of freshly peeled pomegranate seeds, kissed her brother's cheeks and squeezed his hand.

"This would not have been without you," Baal whispered.

Shapash the Sun arrived, enticing as wine in her sleeveless golden gown, the rays of her crown splashing the hall with warmth and light. On her finely muscled arm entered old Father El, dignified, cheeks ruddy, white hair flowing and blue robes shining. Father El nodded and waved at the crowd.

Astarte's black hair reached the floor. Loose as raven's wings and studded with diamonds, Astarte's hair alone was her gown. Baal took the hand of his beloved as reverently as Ashtar, the Water Boy, had taken his own. When she sat down with Baal, the musicians began to play. "Seventy times seventy!" Baal called out in his loudest voice.

"Long may you rule!" his guests shouted.

Baal's wine slid silken down his throat. He looked contentedly at the company.

But a draft suddenly chilled his back. No one else seemed to notice, but a nagging and fearful thought slithered into his peace. In the midst of this plenty, these friends, this triumph, there intruded into

Baal's mind the picture of the one god whom he had not invited. Mot, Drought Maker, King of the Underworld, was not here.

"Yamm the Sea Dragon is gone," Baal told himself. "I must not think of Mot. He doesn't deserve to come." He downed the chalice of wine. Laughter swirled amid the sounds of strings and drums. He reached for Astarte's hand.

"What is it, my love?" asked Astarte, turning her face toward him, her lips full and hennaed.

"Mot," said Baal.

"What?"

"Mot."

"What about him, darling?"

Baal knitted his brow. "Could Mot at this very moment," he asked, "be plotting to take my place as ruler of Earth?"

"Send him a message, darling," said Astarte. "Ashtar!" she called to the Water Boy, who sat near Kothar the Smith. The deities relayed her call until Ashtar came to Astarte's side. "Go, darling, to Mot, and take him this message from Baal."

Ashtar's eyes widened.

"Tell him that Baal is supreme. Tell him that Baal will pay tribute to no one." Astarte smiled, then looked around at Baal. The corners of his beautiful mouth were flat.

"Go!" she said to the Water Boy. She turned to the Prince of Fertility and touched his lips with her fingertips. "Now dance with me," she said into his ear. "All is well."

But Baal gripped her wrist and shouted after the Water Boy, "Ashtar!" The boy stopped. "Ashtar, Mot lives under the mountain with the twin peaks. Lift up the mountain and descend and take my message to Mot. But whatever you do, don't get too near his throne, or he will snatch you like a lamb between his jaws. Tell him I am king."

The boy sped away, and Baal danced with Astarte in his arms.

The party was over and the dining hall empty of all but Baal when Ashtar finally returned. Ashtar knelt among the clutter of plates, goblets, gnawed bones, and seeds sucked clean of their flesh. "What is it, Ashtar?" asked Baal. "What did Mot say?"

"My lord, Mot is angry. He knew about your feast, my lord. He says that if you will not have him as your guest, he will have you. He says that you imagine he has mud and filth to feast on, but that he will heap upon you such fare as you have never tasted before."

Baal again felt the chill at his back. The great hall was silent except for the sound of the boy's breathing and his own.

"I dare not go," he muttered. "Mot will kill me if I go to his palace."

The Water Boy raised his face. "Oh no, my lord. You are King of the World, my lord."

But Baal summoned messengers from the Vineyard and the Meadow. "Flatter Mot and win his favor," he told them. "Bring him the most lavish of your gifts. And tell him that I am his servant, his devoted slave!"

But Mot would not take Baal's gifts. "He says you are a coward, my lord," said the messenger of the Vineyard. "He says you try to insult him and that you have no mettle." The messenger of the Meadow nodded. "He is very angry, my lord. He dares you to come to his table."

Baal saw that he would have to confront his rival. He painted his face with red ocher as a charm against the forces of Death. He rallied the Clouds and the Winds to carry seventy bushels of silver coins as gifts; he placed Driver and Repeller on the seat of his chariot.

Baal heaved up the twin peaks of the mountain. Their soil stayed in his fingernails and streaked his face and robes. The Clouds and the Winds left the gifts of silver coins with the first legion of Mot's guards. Baal strapped Driver and Repeller to his waist and entered a maze of darkling steps that wound deep into the earth. It seemed that Mot's guards had known he was coming, for at each iron gateway they saluted respectfully. Baal grew surprisingly confident as he passed through each of seven gates. The guards' reception was reassuringly friendly.

Even so, he was not prepared for Mot's apparent graciousness. "Baal!" said Mot. His voice was warm and soothing. "You have come so far! You will want to bathe before you eat! I have drawn a bath for you."

Indeed, steam curled from a long tub that crouched on birds' talons. The King of the Underworld's smile was ghastly, and his body under his loose-hanging robes skeletal. Except for his purplish eye sockets and the spots of red on his cheeks, Mot's face was white as lime. His lips were bloodless and his teeth brown and sharp. But his looks stirred in Baal more pity than fear, and he wanted to believe Mot's sincerity.

"He's lonely," Baal thought smugly. "I should have come a long time ago. He is much easier to handle than I thought."

As Baal's eyes grew accustomed to the dimness, he saw beside the tub an iron table on which had been laid a sumptuous feast. He laid down his weapons and gratefully settled himself into the hot water. Soaking in the tub, he found himself enjoying a conversation with his enemy. The days of brooding about his fate slipped away, and his body relaxed. By the time he had emerged from his bath and rested, he found himself ravenously hungry.

Baal forgot that whoever eats of the food of the Underworld may nevermore return to the world above.

Mot's eyes glittered with approval as Baal heaped his plate. When Baal had tasted his first morsel, Mot threw back his head and laughed. "Now you are fully welcomed, my friend!"

Baal felt the sleep of death steal over him. Not even his misjudgment of Mot mattered to him now.

At once, Earth above began to languish. No rain fell, no green thing grew up. The Clouds and the Winds, waiting beside Baal's chariot, looked at each other uneasily. When the corn in the field before them shriveled on its stalks, they raced to the throne of Father El. Breathless and distraught, they fell before him. "Sire! Baal has sunk to the Underworld! We wait for him and he does not return! The fields are dying! There is no rain!"

Old Father El started from his throne. "He has eaten of Mot's table, I know it!" he rasped.

The Clouds and the Winds lay limp before him. "We fear it is so, sire. We fear it so."

Father El ripped away the shoulder of his azure robe. Down he came from his throne and strewed ashes upon his head. "Baal is dead!" he raised his voice in lamentation. Down from his mountain he stumbled, over and over calling his mournful song in the fields and the valleys of Earth. "Baal is dead! Baal is dead!"

"Nooooooooooooo!" screamed Anat, the sister of Baal, when she heard El's words. Like a ewe bereft of its lamb, or a cow its calf, she moaned. She tore her flesh and searched for her brother with a wild and frantic keening.

Shapash the Sun heard her cries. "What is it, Anat?" she asked kindly.

"Lady Sun," Anat said brokenly. "My brother is dead. He never came back from Mot, and I cannot even find his body for a funeral."

Shapash leaned closer. "Is Baal in the Underworld?"

Anat tensed, startled by a sudden hope. "Yes, my lady! Shapash! You are the only one of the gods who can go and return from Mot's realm. Shapash, my lady, will you go and look for Baal and bring him back to me?"

Shapash's face glowed with sympathy. "I will go, Anat. I will return with Baal's body."

Shapash left. Night plunged over the sorrowful Anat, weeping now in relief. Already no green thing grew, and while Shapash searched for Baal, neither did Earth have light.

Shapash finally returned with Baal's body in her arms. The musicians of Baal's party now played dirges, and the gods and goddesses who had danced and feasted now rent their clothes and wept. Sadly, not knowing what else to do, they made Ashtar, the Water Boy, King of the Land. Ashtar's head could not reach the top of Baal's throne, nor could his feet even touch its footstool.

Anat found Mot strolling through the dead fields of Earth. The Prince of Sterility did not even have time to cry out. With a roar of rage, she pushed him to the ground, ripped him into pieces with her sword, burned his flesh in fire, winnowed him with her breath, ground him in a mill, and sowed him into the Earth.

That night the gods and goddesses dreamed dreams of rivers running with honey, of clouds raining soft oil, of green plants bursting with milk. Baal woke from his death as from a sleep, and Shapash took him up again, this time alive, in her arms.

The Lady Sun carried Baal to his palace. Astarte kissed his brow, his ears, and his lips. Ashtar, the Water Boy, climbed down from Baal's throne. Anat washed her brother's feet, fed him, and perfumed his hair. Baal, Prince of Fertility, waxed strong again, and the gods and goddesses rejoiced.

But deep in the Earth, where Anat had sown the pieces of his body, Mot also revived. Out of the Earth Mot sprouted, rising again in his ancient form. "Baaaaaaaaaaaaaaaal!!" he roared. "Come and fight!"

Long and fierce was the battle of the Prince of Death and the Prince of Life. They pranced like antelopes, gored like bulls, charged like stallions, and stung like asps. Now Mot triumphed, now Baal.

At the height of their fury, Shapash the Sun raised her voice. "MOT!" she cried out.

The Prince of Death lay gasping on the ground.

"Mot! Leave Baal to the Upperworld, and return to your own abode," ordered Sun. "The time has come for life. Go, Mot, or every god and goddess will pluck up the foundations of your house and break your scepter."

The light from Sun blinded Mot. Baal stood panting, while Mot, covering his eyes, rose and conceded the fight. "Let Baal be king," said Mot, and turned away.

Baal fell on his face before Shapash the Sun. "I am your servant," said the King of the Rain.

Shapash the Sun smiled. Warmed and strengthened, Baal raised himself up and walked, his step increasingly light, away to his palace. There he would send through his great window the snow, the rain, and the moisture in every right season.

Spider Grandmother Finds Light for Her People

FROM THE KIOWA NATION,
GREAT PLAINS, NORTH AMERICA

The story of Spider Grandmother comes from the Kiowa Nation, once the largest tribe of nomadic peoples on the North American plains. For us, it could be a story about the creative process of coming to a new relationship with solar energy. Like the warrior animals, we may at first be impatient and too narrowly focused. But these modes precede a quiet knowing of the true geography of the task and the beginning of a sure-reflexed persistence.

Spider is a remarkable little being. She grows by shedding her rigid, outer shell. She pulls loose part by part, weak at first, but she soon has the firm skeleton of a new understanding from which to move again.

Like an old woman, Spider is often maligned and given low status in modern culture. Kiowan women participated neither in government nor in the hunt. Like spiders spinning, they performed instead the endless repetitive tasks of life that allow the dramas to unfold. Perhaps the Kiowan storyteller compensated for the glorification of the warrior by making a hero of Spider Grandmother.

Today, the Kiowa, survivors of enormous cultural change, live in the midst of Oklahoma. For centuries, the tribe's core ritual was a regular ten-day festival called the Sun Dance. The Sun Dance enacted a deep human submission to the cycle of life and death. It honored the intimacy between the people and the buffalo, which at the time thundered in herds so large they might take as long as two days to pass a single point.

But European-immigrant settlers coveted buffalo territory for crops and slaughtered the animal in record numbers. Tensions between the whites and the Kiowa reached agonized peaks in the 1870s. By 1887, there were no more buffalo, and the last buffalo-honoring Sun Dance took place.

For a few years around the turn of century, a ritual called the Ghost Dance echoed the Sun Dance. Ghost Dance leaders promised that the ritual would revive the old life, resurrect the dead, and return the buffalo to a renewed earth.

Today, the Kiowa and other tribes unite themselves in the Native American Church. The church mixes Christian symbolism with the ritual use of peyote. Peyote purges the body and induces psycho-spiritual visions for individuals wrestling with the contradictions of life in modern tribal America.

Spider Grandmother Finds Light for Her People

A VERY LONG TIME AGO, the world was young. There was no light. It was night all the time, even in daytime. One dark day, the animals gathered together to complain. "We must have light!" they told one another. "We can't see anything—not even the ground we walk on."

Rabbit held up his foot. "Don't worry any longer," he said. "I will find light." So away Rabbit hopped to find light. But he came back with nothing.

Fox shoved his way to the center of the crowd. "Our people have nothing to fear," said Fox. "The Great Fox is here! I will find light." Then Fox strode off to find light. But Fox came back with his head low. He, too, had not been able to find light.

Then Eagle drew himself up to his full height. When he spoke, all the other animals were quiet. "I will bring my people light," said Eagle. And he soared away on his great wings. But Eagle came back with his wings drooping in discouragement. Eagle could not find light either.

Woodpecker thought he would try his luck. "I-I-I ca-ca-ca-ca-can f-f-f-f-find lie-lie-lie-light," said Woodpecker. But Woodpecker returned as the others had, without light.

The animals continued to complain and brag among themselves. Then suddenly, they heard a tiny voice that sounded very old. "I believe I can bring light to our people," said the voice.

"Who's that?" shouted Fox.

"Yessssss, who sssssaid that?" asked Snake.

"It's Spider Grandmother!" guffawed Fox, slapping his knee.

Eagle put up his wing to hide his beak. Then he threw back his head and laughed. "If even I can't find light, how does Spider Grandmother think she can?" he chortled.

The other animals snickered and chuckled. "Spider Grandmother? Ha! She's too little, and she's way too old."

Well, Spider Grandmother had lived a very long time and she was very wise. So it wasn't that she didn't hear the animals laughing at her. She did hear them. She just didn't pay them much attention.

Instead, she set out on a journey to the Land of the Sun People. She crossed vast deserts. She climbed up high mountains and down their other sides. She walked around huge lakes. All the while she walked, she spun out her thread behind her, so that she would be able to find her way back to her people. She traveled through the dark of many days and the dark of many nights. Once she stopped to make a bowl of some cool clay she had found. Then, carrying her bowl, she pushed on, spinning her thread behind her and moving closer and closer to the Land of the Sun People.

Finally, Spider Grandmother saw an orange glow at the edge of the darkness. It began to turn pink, and Spider Grandmother knew then that she had arrived in the Land of the Sun People. Closer and closer she crept to the huge fire that lit the land of the Sun People. Then quickly and quietly, so quickly and quietly that none of the Sun People noticed her, Spider Grandmother broke off a piece of the fire, put it in her bowl, and began to follow her thread back to her people.

To her surprise, however, the fire in the bowl began to grow. It grew bigger and bigger, and hotter and hotter. It got so hot and so big that Spider Grandmother could stand it no longer. So, small as she was, she hurled the fire into the sky, so high that it stuck. And there it stays to this day, where it is the sun that lights our days.

But Spider Grandmother remembered to save a tiny piece of the fire in her bowl. That piece she took back to her people. That is how the people got fire to cook their food, to bake their bowls hard, and to light their campfires at night.

And that is why, to this very day, when people sit around their campfires at night, they tell stories, like this one, about Spider Grandmother.

Harambee: The Story of the Pull-Together Morning

FROM THE SUKUMA PEOPLE, TANZANIA

Every group of people who has been colonized mentally or physically can attest to the astounding difficulties of their transitions to healing and freedom. African American people, whose roots are in American soil, draw strength for these transitions by exploring Africa's rich, multicultural literatures and ways.

The African American holiday of Kwanza is loosely translated from the Swahili as "first things first." An amalgamation of African language and tribal values with the American struggle for wholeness and the December solstice season, Kwanza celebrates seven principles of struggle and growth in community: Umoja means Unity; Kujichagulia means Self-Determination; Ujima means Collective Work and Responsibility; Ujamaa means Cooperative Economics; Nia means Purpose; Kuumba means Creativity; and Imani means Faith. Kwanza's principles are the same values needed by all of Western culture as we face the economic and ecological tasks of shifting to a directly solar energy base.

Harambee means "pull together" in Swahili. This story from the Sukuma people of Tanzania is a picture of collaboration and canniness in the face of multiple obstacles. It is the story of neighbors joining together because, despite their differences, they all have something to lose and gain in common.

The Sukuma, a chiefdom formed in the 1700s on the south slopes of Lake Victoria, depend in their everyday lives on neighbors rather than on kin. Unlike many Tanzanian peoples who group themselves by direct bloodlines to the same male or female ancestor, Sukuma kin may be widely scattered. Even when kin gather for ritual matters—births, marriages, deaths, ancestral sacrifices—the Sukuma expect their neighbors to participate.

American culture so greatly values "independence" that we feel pressured to deny our need for one another. But we are fed, clothed, sheltered, transported, and our wastes carried away by an orchestra of other people. Other people's thoughts, inventions, and works form and guide us. Friends, as often as relatives, are the precious mainstays of our sense of well-being. The psychological solstices in our lives require us to celebrate our dependence on one another.

But the web of our lives has ecological as well as social strands. Before the 1600s, in Western culture's "Wood Age," everything from shoes to buckets to printing presses was made of wood. People met their energy needs by gathering and burning sticks and logs. Green plants miraculously produced food, shelter, and fuel. Although people didn't use the word photosynthesis, they understood that green plants needed the sun to grow. So people honored as spiritual kin the earth, the trees, and the sun.

But in the 1600s, Europe entered her first major energy crisis. The Law of Entropy proved itself when Europe ran out of wood. To meet the energy needs of her burgeoning population, Europe was forced to enter the "Coal Age." And Newton's new science of world-as-machine began to chop away at our mythic ties to our spiritual kin in the natural world.

Today, supplies of coal have dropped sharply. Entropy has forced us to enter the "Oil and Nuclear Ages," in which the procurement of new energy sources itself takes astounding amounts of energy. But oil reserves are limited. Nuclear technology is so wasteful that it has been compared to using a power saw to cut butter. Moreover, its waste products are deadly.

All energy comes to us through plants—or through the animals that eat plants. Plants get their life directly from the sun. Technology, however, has obscured our relationship with the plants that feed and fuel us all. Honoring the earth, plants, and sun as our kinfolk may seem quaint today, but these dependencies form the basis for our survival and are the hidden center of all other cultural practices.

Harambee: The Story of the Pull-Together Morning

A T THE BEGINNING OF THE world, there was no sun in the sky. Everyone was falling into holes, bumping into one another, and picking a lot of fights.

Lion called a meeting of all the people. Everyone came: Giraffe, Zebra, Antelope, Monkey, Cobra. They jostled and bickered with one another for a long time before Crocodile finally got their attention.

"Listen, people!" said Crocodile. "Umoja. If we're going to solve our problems, we've got to admit that despite our differences, we're all in this together."

Antelope broke the sober silence that followed Crocodile's words. "Harambee," she said. "We've got to pull together."

"Yes!" shouted someone else. "Harambee! We've got to pull together."

The crowd repeated it. "Harambee," they said. "Harambee!"

Then Leopard began the problem solving. "Sometimes when it rains," he suggested, "the sky cracks open. You know how you can see a blaze of light on the other side of the crack? If only we could get to the other side of the sky and get some of that light for ourselves!"

Hyena laughed. "How are we supposed to get up there?" she asked.

"Even if we could get up there, we're too big to get through the crack," Elephant pointed out.

Mouse nudged Spider and tapped Fly's wing. "*We're* not too big," she whispered. Then in a loud voice she offered, "Spider, Fly, and I will try."

The people murmured hopeful approval.

"Wait a second," said Fly. "I can't go with Spider."

"You're forgetting!" cried Monkey. "Harambee! We've got to pull together!"

"But she'll eat me!" moaned Fly.

"Imani," said Spider firmly. "Have faith, Fly. Why would I eat you when you're helping us all get light?"

Fly was silent.

"Harambee," said Mouse. "We've got to pull together."

Fly thoughtfully rubbed two of his back legs together. Finally, he said, "Okay. I'll go."

The big animals cheered. "And we'll stay right here and make music for you until you return," announced Lion.

"Harambee!" everyone shouted. "Harambee!"

Spider spun a silver ladder to the top of the sky. Mouse and Fly climbed carefully after her. With her sharp little teeth, Mouse gnawed a hole in the sky at the end of the ladder and the three small animals squeezed themselves through to the land of the Sky People.

They blinked and looked at one another in the new light. Mouse's whiskers bristled delicately and Fly's wings glittered purple and green. They could hear a faint surge of sound from the people below.

Spider smiled. "We did it!" she said.

"Harambee," said Mouse. "We're pulling together."

Everywhere around them in a shining grass field were the Sky People moving swish, swish, to and fro.

The Sky People curiously questioned their strange visitors and then took Mouse, Fly, and Spider to their king. "These people want light," they told the king. "They say they've come from Earth to get it."

Now the King of the Sky People did not want to give these strangers light. But he also did not wish to appear ungenerous. He shifted on his throne, adjusted his bright robes, and pressed his fingertips together. "This is not a small matter," he said importantly. "I must call a meeting."

Spider, Mouse, and Fly watched as the Sky People gathered behind the vibrant black, red, and green folds of a big tent. Fly winked at his companions, then flew toward the secret council.

The people inside talked long and seriously. But they never noticed Fly, who had taken a place very quietly on the wall. "We can't give these people light," said the king. "We'll give them a test instead. They won't be able to pass it—and then I can have them killed."

The king pushed back the beautiful cloth and Fly flew quickly to Spider and Mouse. "He's going to try to kill us," Fly whispered.

"We're going to have to pull together," said Spider.

"Harambee," murmured Mouse.

"Friends," said the king to the three small animals. "My people need grass for their roofs. You may have light if—and only if—you cut down all the grass in this field by morning." The king smiled smugly.

Mouse smiled back. "Thank you for your generosity, oh King. We will do it."

"What do you mean, 'we'll do it'?" cried Fly, when the king had gone away. "We're never going to be able to cut all that grass."

"Harambee," said Spider. "Harambee."

Mouse thought for a moment. "Yes!" she said. "Harambee! I'll be right back." Mouse wiggled back through the hole in the sky and down the silver ladder. Soon she returned in the company of the Ants, who had been making music at the bottom. They marched, feelers keeping time to the drumbeats far below. "Harambee!" yelled the Queen of the Ants, and by morning not a single stalk of grass stood in the field.

The king looked uncomfortable, but he pretended to be pleased. "Ah," he said. "Yes. Well, I see you've passed the first test. But now, of course," the king paused and pressed his fingertips together. "You must pass another. I will kill a cow. And you must eat all the meat by morning."

The Sky People brought basket after basket of freshly roasted meat. "Thank you for your generosity, good people," said Spider. Fly buzzed with anticipation.

"But even I can't eat all that," he said sadly, when the Sky People had gone away.

"The big animals could in a second," said Mouse.

"Yeah, but how are they supposed to get up here?" asked Spider.

"This is impossible," said Fly, sucking a bit of meat to comfort himself.

"Imani," said Spider. "Have faith, Fly."

"Hey! I've got an idea!" said Mouse.

The three friends looked at one another. "Harambee," they said.

Mouse dug long tunnels in the ground. Fly and Spider helped Mouse bury the meat in the tunnels. In the morning, not one scrap of meat lay in the baskets. Fly, Spider, and Mouse thanked the king for the delicious feast.

The king pursed his lips. He did not look happy, but he managed to smile. "Congratulations," he said. "Since you've passed the second test, I must call another meeting."

Spider and Mouse waited outside while Fly once again took his silent place on the wall.

The king was furious. "These little people are strong," he fumed. "I can see we're going to have to give them light. But I'm going to make it hard for them."

Fly flew back and told his friends the king's plan. "He's got two boxes," explained Fly. "The black one has darkness in it. The red box has light. He's going to make us pick."

Just then, the king burst through the curtain with the two boxes. "You must choose," he said. He narrowed his eyes and traded the boxes from one hand to the other. "Light or dark?" He raised his eyebrows and waited.

Mouse pretended to think. "Hmmm," she said. Then, quickly, before the king could change his mind, she grabbed the red box and raced for the hole in the sky. Mouse, Spider, and Fly plunged down the silver ladder into the waiting, music-making crowd below.

"They have returned!" roared Lion. "They've returned!"

"They're back!" the people yelled excitedly.

Mouse's whiskers trembled a little. "We've pulled together—all of us," she said in her loudest voice. "And we've brought you light—in this box!"

The crowd hushed when Spider and Fly pushed up the lid on the red box. But out of the box came not light at all. Instead, Rooster jumped out of the box. He picked up one foot, then the other, and rustled his feathers handsomely.

Mouse felt her cheeks grow hot. Rooster was not light! She had been tricked by the Sky King! The people began to protest.

At that moment, Rooster threw back his head. "Ha-ha-ha-ram-beeeee!" he called out. "Ha-ha-ha-ram-beeeee!" At once the eastern sky filled with color. Pink and yellow it glowed, and then the sun popped fiery red into the sky.

That's how it was on that very first golden, pull-together morning. And Rooster has been calling up the sun for all of us ever since—"Ha-ha-ha-ram-beeeee!"

Baubo's Dance

The many-faceted movement called feminism is repositioning modern culture's relationship to gender and the earth. Whether or not we call ourselves feminists, more and more of us are exploring ways to mix our sexualities with our spiritualities and our psychologies with our ecologies. As usual, myths are our guides. Since modern Western culture has strong mythic roots in ancient Greece, Greek myths provide peculiarly compelling maps.

The usual telling of the Greek myth of Demeter and Persephone is a poignant picture of the sadness we feel during the winters of our lives. With charming contrasts, it is also similar to the Ugaritic story of Shapash the Sun (see "How Shapash the Sun Rescued the Prince of Fertility"). Demeter, queen of all green, plays the ancient Semitic prince of fertility. Hades, though unnamed in this telling, is the lord of the Greek underworld who kidnaps Demeter's daughter, Persephone. Hades plays the part of Mot, prince of death. Persephone, like Baal, eats of the food in the underworld and is thus made a prisoner there.

This myth is enjoying renewed popularity, and much reinterpretation, in women's discussions about psycho-spirituality. It is the story of the feminine obliged to live in the underworld while another part of her searches for the release that will green the world again.

In this unusual version of the tale, the old woman Baubo dances erotically for Demeter, causing her to laugh. Demeter's laughter encourages Helios the Sun to emerge from his seclusion, and Persephone to begin her ascent from the underworld. The trinity of crone-mother-maiden is the Greek answer to the Kiowan Spider Grandmother (see "Spider Grandmother Finds Light for Her People"). Baubo is the wizened old woman. Mother Demeter carries Spider Grandmother's per-

sistence. Maiden Persephone takes Spider Grandmother's long, dark journey.

Only to the modern Westerner, accustomed to the automatic desexualization of the old woman, does the picture of mother-maiden sexuality seem complete. The crone Baubo, at first, seems grotesque as a fairytale witch, the antithesis of sexuality as commonly defined by Western culture. But an ancient Greek artist carved Baubo simply as a face on a pubic triangle above a woman's legs. Baubo, the dancing hag, represents the erotic we have hidden away. She personifies a pan-eroticism born of delight and awe for body and earth. In a similar personification, Ame-no-Uzume, another crone, danced erotically for the Japanese Mother Sun Amaterasu Omikami.

The classicist Edith Hamilton added Helios the Sun to the story of Demeter, Persephone, and Baubo. Sun's emergence begins Persephone's spring. Helios, in this story, has already lost his son, Phaethon, who insisted on driving his father's fiery chariot. Phaethon, like Icarus, who flew too close to the sun and melted the wax on his wings, was full of the longing and hubris of youth and did not survive his high ride.

Baubo's Dance

ONCE UPON A TIME, THE
earth dressed all the year
in tendriling green. Helios the
Sun rose early every morning
and delayed his bedtime as long as possible to be able to talk and
laugh with the two great goddesses below. Demeter, queen of all green
plants, and her fawn-eyed daughter, Persephone, played in an endless
spring and summer.

But one terrible day, Persephone was stolen underground. Demeter mourned. Helios the Sun hid himself away. Fall and winter came
to the land. Demeter searched for her daughter and found Baubo instead. Because of Baubo, Demeter laughed and Helios shone again.
Only then was Persephone able to return to the upperworld.

It happened like this.

One day Persephone said good-bye to Demeter. The girl's lips felt
like petals on her mother's cheek. "Be careful," said Demeter, without

knowing why. There should be no danger, after all, for goddesses in an endless spring and summer. But a strange fear stabbed Demeter's heart.

"I will, Mama, I will," said Persephone, as she skipped away. Demeter watched her lickety-split the meadow until she was only a mark in the distance.

Persephone wandered and wondered that day. She fingered the skirts of the poppies that blew in the bee-buzzed grasses. She scattered dandelion fuzz. Farther away, she drank from a cool pond and studied with solemn eyes her face in its blue mirror. With her fingertips, she touched her full lips. She lowered and raised her lashes. She stroked her neck for a moment, then left off, sighing. Then, she gazed for a long time at something beneath her face in the pool. Finally, she dreamed against a hot red rock while the scent of narcissus rose thick around her.

Suddenly, a man rode a horse from the center of the earth. The animal's nostrils distended over his soft mouth, and the black-garbed man swung himself down to talk to the startled girl. His words first relaxed her. She lingered, and then his words began to probe. Her voice grew coy. Her breath grew eager and she felt her heart pound.

Demeter saw none of this. She heard only the scream. When she rushed to look for her child, she found only a crumpled shoe next to the giant red rock. The grass around it was trampled as though there had been a struggle. Demeter could find her daughter nowhere, and Persephone did not come home. It was Helios who told her that Persephone had been stolen away to the underworld. The fear in Demeter's heart changed to terror. Helios, remembering his own lost child, turned away in sorrow.

Demeter could not stop hearing her daughter's scream. The next morning she could not move. Helios had to struggle to get out of bed. Darkened days stuttered by, and the world withered without the attention of the queen of all green and of Helios the Sun. Trees lost their leaves, wheat and barley shriveled on the stalk, fruits withered and shrunk away to dry pits. Helios hid himself, and snow covered everything but old Baubo's house. Baubo, friend of the animals, baked, spun, and sipped tea in her house nestled in a valley.

The animals, not wanting to starve, began a trek to Baubo's house. They scurried, scuttled, and shivered. They clambered in and out of the deep white drifts.

Baubo opened her house to them all.

Finally, even in the dark, Demeter found her way to Baubo's house in the valley. By the glow from its windows, she could see the tangle of anise and roses on the roof. She could smell vanilla orchids fermenting at its windows. Suddenly, a gust of warm purple air billowed and lifted Demeter, tattered and spattered with mud, all the way to the latch.

The door swung open. Inside, a skinny, old woman offered her an apple.

"I am Baubo, my pretty one," she rasped, "and this is for you."

Demeter did not take the apple, but she allowed herself to be steadied over the doorsill. She could smell the old woman's breath, sweet as anise and vanilla. By the light of the beeswax tapers, the old woman's breasts hung low in her blouse. Her irises, though frosted with white, glowed. Hairs bristled on her chin.

Baubo put the apple on the plank of the table while Demeter sat in a stupor on a stool. She felt swaddled by the yeasty steam drifting from the belly of a black oven. Baubo set before her a bowl of porridge. Sitting in a chair, she watched Demeter spoon it as a child would, not caring for the drips. Cupboards and a bed piled with quilts and round pillows hulked in the shadows.

Finally, Demeter wiped her mouth on her sleeve and looked up.

"It's time to talk," said the old woman.

Demeter put on the table her daughter's shoe. She fidgeted with its edges, then began to cry quietly. Slowly, relief filled her at the prospect of laying the burden of her pain before this grandmother. She told about the good-bye, the scream, the matted grass at the side of the red rock, about Persephone's not coming back. She told how the sun had gone away, how the ice and snow had come, how she had traveled here to this house in the valley. Tears dripped from her chin.

Baubo's mouth had been still as she listened. Now it twitched. She reached for the shoe. Muttering with effort, she drew from the cavern of its toe a knife. The blade glinted in the candle flames. Knife and shoe now lay on the table next to the apple.

Demeter's eyes widened. She searched Baubo's face.

Then out of the corners, out of the cupboards, creeping from under the bed, came a wild, alive hatching of the whole room. Three swallows swooped from the rafters. A beaver bared his teeth and slapped his tail beside a bucket. A weasel nosed open the lower shelf of a cupboard. Four squirrels chattered on the windowsill. The pillows on the bed uncurled as serpents, hissing and curving from side to side. Animals rose up everywhere and a music began. A mole shuffled. Two deer clacked antlers. Six rabbits thumped. Three starlings cackled. From behind the bed, a wolf pointed her nose to the ceiling and bayed. A bear stamped back and forth before the black-bellied stove. Clusters of bees swarmed overhead.

Baubo wagged her head and peppered the table with her fingers and palms. She pushed herself up. She cut her eyes at the bear. She patted her feet. She flicked her skirt at the fox. She parted her blouse for a mink. Slowly, hair, breasts, and limbs undulating, Baubo began to dance.

The animals drummed.

Baubo swayed her hips. She picked up her feet. She showed her back, turned her front. Sweat beaded her lip.

With a flicker of the first hope she'd felt in weeks, Demeter surprised herself by standing up.

Baubo shrugged away her blouse. The rhythm climbed. Baubo whirled and with one hand gathered her skirts to her waist.

Demeter's stomach jumped when a scar showed purple on Baubo's belly.

Baubo twirled and arched her neck.

A sudden rush of energy filled Demeter, and her lips parted.

Baubo danced her thighs open and touched the wisps of her hair. She closed her teeth over her lower lip, flirted her eyes at Demeter, and humped.

Demeter laughed.

Baubo chortled.

Demeter snatched up the knife, decision jutting her jaw. She split the apple into two creamy, starred halves, and then slit the rags from her body. The knife clattered to the floor, and she reached for the hand of the hag. Their two hands seized, and the house in the valley sobbed with sound.

Away in the distance, Helios the Sun shook his head, not sure if he'd heard correctly. The music swelled and Helios nodded, wonder and hope in his heart. He stepped to his door.

Inside the house in the valley, Baubo and Demeter tipped back their throats and whooped.

Helios shook his head and smiled. Then he walked into the sky.

Sunlight peeked in through the windows of the house in the valley. It glanced off the brown apple seeds. It lit the bear's wet snout and shivered in the mole's whiskers.

Down the road, icicles cracked loudly on tree branches and broke away.

A huge red rock above the valley trembled as someone heaved it aside from underneath.

Web of Fear: The Story of Akewa the Sun and Jaguar Man

FROM THE TOBA PEOPLE,
GRAN CHACO REGION, ARGENTINA

A story as strange and raw as this one seems to have little to do with modern relationships between women and men. Today, women and men enjoy more freedom from gender-typing than ever before in Western cultural history. Our visions for equality are sophisticated. Yet we seem obliged to find our ways to each other through a passionate morass of curiosity, fear, rage, and hope. This story chronicles the joy and agony of intimacy between the genders. It is a mythic snapshot of our compassion-threaded misunderstandings.

The story comes from the Toba, who live on the swampy, hot, subtropical plain of northern Argentina. A subgroup of one of the region's four great nomadic tribes, the Toba have lived in the Gran Chaco region for possibly thousands of years. The Gran Chaco is a region sometimes blistering, sometimes wet, and filled with blood-sucking insects. When European immigrants first arrived, they were amazed at the survival skills of the Toban warriors, who were also collectors of wild fruits, nuts, and honey. The abundant growth of the region's quebracho, *or "ax-breaker," tree attracted colonizers because of its extraordinary durability and its high levels of cowhide-curing tannin. Struggles between the Gran Chaco's nomads and their colonizers lasted for more than three hundred years. To this day, the first peoples of the Gran Chaco maintain separate racial and cultural identities from the rest of Argentina's peoples.*

Like other mythologies in the South American continent, the Toban mythology makes much of catastrophe and is concerned with contradictory states of existence. Flood, fire, drought, earthquake, putrefaction, and petrification fill these tales. The Toban world was cocreated by the Evil One and the Good One. Kaloarai'k filled the creation with suffering and woe; Peritnali'k taught the wordless magical chants that overcame the horrors. For the Toba, the human body is a mythic landscape. In the center of the chest live individual guardian spirits who protect against the dangerous, often snake-shaped spirits of the external world.

In the Toban tribe, the central adulthood initiation is for women. In the rite, the young men form a circle around the girls to be initiated. They dance around them, wearing masks of serpents, parrots, winds, and monkeys. Finally, they impersonate bloody-mouthed jaguars and lash the girls' loins with pieces of cloth.

The jaguar, a predator vested with great power and respect, figures in much of South American mythology. The jaguar's actual ability to scent the blood of menstruating women, thus endangering the women and their companions, probably helped form the first human focus on the monthly bleeding of women. In places without artificial light, the menstrual cycle is also mysteriously matched to the moon's pattern of wax and wane. Thus, menstruation, powerful enough to attract the jaguar and the moon in an increasingly predictable rhythm, must almost have seemed to "create" the world again and again (see Judy Grahn's Blood, Bread and Roses).

The Toban girl initiates, as do all groups of women who live together long enough, have synchronized menstrual cycles. The young men flailing them are "helping" to bring their blood, and thus to "create"— once again—the world. Indeed, the harder the times, the greater the need for world-creation magic, and the harder the blows. The "attack" continues until, one by one, each young woman "falls dead," her breasts ritually sucked by her male counterpart.

Akewa, the Toban Sun, is one of a type of culture- and fire-giving celestial women in South American traditions. She has the bizarre "vagina dentata"—or toothed vagina—of mythological fame. The Toba imagine Akewa's vagina as the breeding ground for the piranha fish. Since female genitalia are actually one of the softest of anatomical parts, the image of a toothed vagina seems a metaphor for the power of the harsh mother earth, who gives birth to so much that is fearful and dangerous in the

Gran Chaco. The bloody, toothy mouth of the jaguar is also connected metaphorically to the vagina: the hunting cat (along with wild dogs) was attracted to the blood, and this forced menstruating women to hide themselves away or risk attack. The mystery of a woman's bleeding, her ability to attract danger, and her wondrous capacity to give life, endowed women themselves with fearful power, like the very land on which they lived. The profoundly contradictory image of the toothed vagina mirrors the ambivalence that the power of earth and of woman engenders in us. Humans feel respect and fear in relationship to earth; men feel it in relationship to women. When Philip Roth, in Portnoy's Complaint, describes the penis as a "battering ram to freedom," he presents a similarly ambivalent image. The vulnerability of the male genital is as completely hidden by its picture as a weapon as the tenderness of the vagina is obscured by its picture as a devouring mouth.

Web of Fear: The Story of Akewa the Sun and Jaguar Man

BECAUSE THE LOVE OF Akewa the Sun and Jaguar Man was webbed with fear from the very beginning, they still travel alone, meeting only occasionally, and then with ferocity.

So fascinated were Akewa and Jaguar Man with each other that they became, as objects of each other's desires, also frightened of the other's power. Even at the moments of greatest sweetness in each other's arms, they were haunted by the rumors they themselves had begun, which claimed that each of them had too many teeth.

At the beginning, Akewa lived with her sister sky women in the heavens, all of them fat and round and beautiful, all of them graceful and given to laughter. They sat in their blue sky room, braiding one another's blazing hair and drinking great pitchers of *yerba mate* from black iron cups.

Jaguar Man lived on the earth below with his brothers among the eye-glowing circles of fire borrowed from the sisters in the sky. All the jaguar brothers were sleek and supple and were mated only to the great quiet hunt.

The sisters had lent the men fire; they had lowered it down on a rope from the sky; they had slipped it down with a song and a coyness so skin-tingling that the brothers rose up as one and peered, hearts pounding, into the heavens.

The sisters, held in the gaze of the jaguar men, blushed furiously. How suddenly compelling were these dark creatures on the earth below! How thrilling were the magnets of their eyes; how soft their furs looked; how musical their purrs!

The sky sisters tittered and whooped. They teased one another to follow the fire down the rope and join the jaguar men below. They invented stories of who would be partnered with whom, poured more *yerba mate,* and made much of the patterns of the leaves in the bottoms of their cups.

Only round, radiant Akewa held herself apart. She watched her sisters pulsing brilliantly against the soft blue of the walls of their home. She hated the terrible change she saw coming.

The thin voices of the men below began to float up the rope. "Come down," said the voices. "Come for a visit," they called. Some of the brothers tried to climb the rope, but none could manage higher than the first bank of clouds.

The sisters dissolved again into pillows of giggles.

Akewa shouted at them, "Stop it! Shut up! Don't you see that these creatures have monstrous teeth? Their mouths are cavernous weapons—when they're not looking up at you, they are tearing apart their prey. What makes you think you are different from what they hunt? What makes you think you can go for a visit and not get eaten alive?"

"They've got teeth?" asked the sky sisters.

"Yes. Teeth," said Akewa. "You go down there, you'll never come back."

The sisters, at first, listened to Akewa the Sun. They turned their backs on the creatures below. But the flirtation had begun, and it was not so easily stopped. Moreover, Akewa's warning of danger added spice to the attraction.

The brothers also had one among them who held back. The strongest and boldest, Jaguar Man wanted only the fraternity of his fellows. "What do you want with these sky women?" he argued. "Yes, they may be fat and beautiful, but they don't have just one mouth like we do—they have another one between their legs. That one is also studded with teeth. What you think will bring you pleasure will be your ruin. They will devour you! They will never be satisfied."

The idea of two mouths, both studded with teeth, on each of the sun sisters gave the jaguar men pause.

"But what good is our strength, Jaguar Man," asked the brothers, "if we cannot subdue them and make them happy?"

Batting one another with their paws and flexing their muscles, the jaguar brothers made ready to receive visitors. They built huts and with the wonderful new fire they roasted whole lizards beneath the house of the sun sisters. The smell of the barbecue wafted upward and made the mouths of the sky sisters water. The brothers brewed *algaroba*-fruit beer and enlisted the help of Falcon for the hour of the sisters' arrival.

Akewa begged them not to go. But the sisters, giddy with daring, laughing and shouting, merely kissed her and told her not to spoil their fun.

One by one, they climbed down the rope. Akewa watched sullenly as they left. But she let out a bellow of rage when she saw Falcon.

Falcon soared to the top of the heavens, and just as Akewa's last sister touched the earth with her feet, Falcon grabbed the rope with his claws and cut it with his beak. Reeling like a giant snake, the rope tumbled forever out of the heavens.

The sisters were trapped.

Staring in agony at the earth, Akewa's hair turned white. She moaned and turned away. Barely able to drag herself along, Akewa, shining alone up in the heavens, made a painfully slow journey across the sky and lowered herself into the abyss at the end of the world.

Down on the earth, each sister walked into the arms of a waiting brother. Everyone sang wild, wordless songs. Only Jaguar Man remained alone, gloomily watching the festivities. So tumultuous was that first meeting, what with the feasting, the rattles, and the mingling, that the sisters did not notice the rope limp and frayed on the ground.

In the long months that followed, lit each day by the grieving old Akewa in the sky, the sisters, sobered in their imprisonment, came nevertheless to live well with their captors. Indeed, the pleasure and intensity of the companionship of the men softened the longing they had for the sky world. But some say the broken rope lies always coiled in the hearts of women, ever after making difficult the complete trust of men.

The heart of Jaguar Man was also sorely troubled. Silently, telling himself that Akewa was just another two-mouthed sister with too many teeth, he nonetheless began to watch her. Something about her long, weary walk each day, something about her ancient face, filled him with pain instead of fear.

Day after day, Akewa walked, caring for nothing except the descent into the dark at the end of each journey. For it was in the beautiful blackness that Akewa felt the ropes of love that tied her to her sisters loosen and begin to unwind. Gradually, so subtlely that she did not know at first she was doing so, she began to braid with those unwound strands a ladder that reached to the lone Jaguar Man, whose green eyes seemed to burn with a sorrow like her own.

Akewa and Jaguar Man began to meet in the dark under the rim of the world. Strange that two so certain and firm were now so wondering and curious. Indeed, Akewa, who had grown so old, grew young again in Jaguar Man's arms. The days on earth shortened as Akewa now hurried across the sky to meet her lover.

Their time together grew and grew until one long night, laughing shyly, they counted each other's teeth and told each other the story of their fears.

Some say Akewa was reborn that night. "I feel like a little child," she told her lover. Jaguar Man traced her eyebrows with his glowing eyes.

Would that the cycle froze itself here at the point of joy! But the cycle does not end here, and neither does our story.

It's true that Akewa is born every year, and then walks, a plump quick child, away from the winter solstice. Slowly she grows older, until she is the grieving, aged one of midsummer, and then she grows younger again, becoming the maiden who once, so long ago, let Jaguar Man climb her rope ladder of love.

But all too often Jaguar Man and Akewa begin to argue. They fight about the hours they meet and leave each other. Earth people see clouds steal away the morning and evening light. They fight about their need to be alone and the merits of their siblings. Perhaps Jaguar Man is again afraid of the woman with two mouths. Might she not be hiding teeth of which she has not told him? And Akewa, perhaps, shrinks from Jaguar Man's wide mouth; how can she be sure he will not use his teeth against her?

Round, fat, and beautiful, Akewa carries weapons across the sky each day. The people on earth see them as her rays, but Jaguar Man sees them stab at that precariously swaying ladder of love, and rage coils in his heart.

Jaguar Man swallows Akewa during the time that people on earth call "eclipse." But her weapons are strong, and Jaguar Man is forced to spit out his burning-hot Akewa.

And so Akewa most often walks alone on her sky journey, old and slow in the dry season, young and quick in the wet. Because the love of Akewa and Jaguar Man was webbed with fear from the very beginning, they meet only occasionally, and then with ferocity.

Surya the Sun's Marriage to Bright and Shadow

FROM HINDU INDIA

This is the story of the solstice we call menarche. *A girl bleeding for the first time stands squarely between the adult world and her childhood. Each month, a woman's bleeding invites her into the quiet shadows of her life. More and more women and their daughters are daring to inhabit this place of contemplation and renewal. They are studying their "periods" as if they were forgotten rubies, transforming the modern Western notion that menstruation is a mere scientific, soulless, or even negative function. Menstruation may no longer be simply an inconvenience to be endured as "sanitarily" as possible. Instead, women are inventing tiny rites that celebrate their bleeding times as spiritually meaningful respites from the secular grind.*

Even today, when a Hindu maiden reaches maturity she is kept in a dark room for four days and forbidden to see the sun. In the Tantric tradition, a woman's cycle has four stages: virginal (Kumari) just after her bleeding; the young wife (Saraswati) during the week following menstruation; the worldly mistress of the house (Lakshmi) during the next week; and the wise lady (Kali) during the approach to her bleeding. During menstruation, she is beyond worldliness, dead to the world and its responsibilities. Across cultures, menstrual seclusion is known as "entrance into the shade."

Healing and balancing rituals for women and men all over the world are essentially reenactments of old menstrual rites. They require a cloistering away—from others, from light, from noise, from responsibility, from ordinary food and activity. The person who periodically secludes him- or herself, like the quietly waiting menstruater, is returned to the place of the forming of the world.

This story of Surya the Sun and his marriage to Bright and Shadow is from the Hindu tradition. Like an instructor who invents still another explanation of a puzzle while her students wrinkle their noses in consternation, Hindu myths offer a kaleidoscope of image and plot so that we might glimpse the charming and terrifying mysteries of the cosmos. Hundreds of deities, thousands of demons, endlessly overlapping personifications of creators, destroyers, and tricksters—countless stories within stories—all are encoded in the lofty hymns of the Vedas and the plainer dialogues of the Puranas.

Surya the Sun was originally a beautiful girl-bride whose magical red "milk" created the world. Blood—back in the times before electricity, plastic, frozen foods, and freeways—pouring out in birth, violence, and the rhythmical clottings of women, seemed truly the maker not just of individual human life but of the very order of the world. When people noticed that the monthly bleeding of women appeared to match exactly the comings and goings of the moon, they began that quintessentially human activity of counting and measure, which became useful much later for written records of food quantity and distribution.

But, as Judy Grahn theorizes in her Blood, Bread and Roses: How Menstruation Created the World, *the first sense of number was probably much more mystical. Rhythmic periods of moon and blood seemed to actually cause light and life itself. Careful measurement of cycles, and the protection and seclusion of the women who seemed to be in charge of the precious mystery, formed the basis of human work and thought. Humans helped to "re-create" the world through a myriad of cultural activities and artifacts: the seclusion ritual (for the protection of the women who kept blood's life power); the chair (a throne of honor for the bleeder); the round-shaped container (copying the shapes of the moon and the sun); even* cosmetics (from the word kosmos, *meaning order), the often brilliantly red decorative paints that recall the color of life-giving blood.*

In the sixth century C.E., *Persian and East European storytellers, steeped in stories of the Roman male sun, Mithra (see introduction to "The Christmas Story"), changed Surya the Sun to male, dressing the* girl-bride in the fiery mantle of a majestic and kindly king. Perhaps, as Judy Grahn suggests, this shift from female to male power was less malignant than simply an attempt to pass women's life-blood mysteries to the men of the culture.

Surya, the boy-man sun, recalls his female origin and his connection to menstrual blood when he is miscarried by his mother, Aditi, the great cosmic cow, in the form of a reddish, misshapen lump. The little clot boy becomes the Sun who marries two women, Bright Image and her sister, Shade. Together, the two sisters are metaphors for the cyclical periods of extroversion and introversion experienced by all humans. Honor for the introverted part of the cycle, so easily ignored or discounted in modern culture, was first practiced in ancient, seclusionary menstrual rites.

The mysterious Shaya, Sister Shadow, Sister Shade, is the image of menstrual introversion in this story. We are not told where she comes from, so I have taken the liberty of having Prajapati Visvakarmen, the smith of the universe, invent her, thus making him, as it were, the father of menstruation. As we examine old gender conceptions and invent new ones, the "patriarchal father" in all of us begins to forge new ways of thinking. We are learning to acknowledge that light, consciousness, and spit-spot orders are only a tiny fraction of the whole cosmos. All begins and exists within the great dark.

Surya the Sun's Marriage to Bright and Shadow

O N THE GREAT LOOM OF the world, held up by the six giant pegs at the ends of the rainbows, the Maiden Night lays out the warp of life and the Maiden Dawn shuttles through the woof. Together they weave the fabric of the eons, and this is the story they tell.

One morning, Prajapati Visvakarmen, smith of the universe, and breath to all that lives, patted his huge blue belly and left his house to look for his cow. But lo! He found he could not reach that heavenly cow, Aditi, vessel of all. She was imprisoned in a fanged and feathered cloud of darkness. He could hear her sadly lowing—but not a one of his seven smithing tools could pry her free. He caught with his thumb a fat blue tear that dripped down his cheek.

The sages and the serpents and the nymphs of heaven perceived Prajapati's sadness. "Why do you mourn?" they sang.

"Aditi is trapped in the dark," moaned Prajapati Visvakarmen, "and I cannot free her."

So the sages and the serpents and the nymphs of heaven began to sing. They sang song and hymn, hymn and song, chanting and currying their music with joy. They sang of Aditi, fat and milky, mild, gracious, sweetly odorous. They sang of Aditi until the feathers of her jail whirled apart and the fangs lost their bite. Then Aditi, vessel of all, stepped forth.

Prajapati Visvakarmen blew out, in his gladness, an ocean of billowing air and set Aditi on it as on a field of blue, tender grass.

Aditi, that heavenly cow, lowed with happiness and chewed the cud of infinite space. Then she poured from her udder a molten butter of light and filled the chest of heaven and earth with treasures.

Prajapati Visvakarmen, watching with tears of pleasure on his cheeks, slapped his belly with sheer delight. Then Aditi lay down on the blue field of heaven and birthed eight sons.

The sages and serpents and nymphs of heaven gathered and sang. Seven sons were born whole and well. But lo! The eighth she miscarried, and he came out an eggish, reddish lump.

Oh! Oh! Oh! The seven tawny brothers groaned with sorrow and sympathy for their poor little brother. The sages and serpents and nymphs of heaven wrung out dirges, and Aditi's huge brown eyes dripped out tears that mixed with the tears of the seven sobbing brothers. Seas welled up; rivers and mountain torrents poured over the earth, all from the tears of the family of the little lump boy.

But then! Lo! The seven brothers washed their egg brother in their tears. They bathed him in their saliva. How they rejoiced when a dark red boy formed himself under their tongues! A little boy with three beautiful eyes and four chubby arms nestled on a red lotus, rays of winged glory spreading from his body.

The song of the sages and serpents and nymphs of heaven soared. Aditi's eyes grew wet this time with pride. "You've made the sun, my children," she lowed. "We'll call him Surya." And the sages and serpents and nymphs of heaven caroled his name.

The dusky red boy's hair grew long and radiant as flames. His brothers made him a crib cozy with clouds. They kissed his hands and tickled his chest. They gave him water lilies to play with.

Then the doting brothers borrowed Prajapati's seven tools and fashioned for their Surya a chariot nine thousand leagues long. Its wheels were the shape of time: every hub a season, every spoke a day.

"Giddyap!" crowed Surya, and his brothers changed themselves to seven bay horses, clattering the car across the heavens while the little sun boy shrieked with excitement.

Surya grew huge and strong. He could lift the clouds with a finger; he protected the stars with his hand. His words and breath, like sweet warm butter, salved the aches of the creatures on earth. Every day, Surya guided his brothers, those magnificent, delicately nostriled horses, as they drew his chariot across the sky. The snakes of heaven lent their long sleek bodies for his reins. Everywhere Surya delivered food; he poured his hot fat light into every form; over the sides of the chariot he sprayed long threads of light to which every being with a mother clung. The oldest sages, Alert and Watchful, sang his praises and the nymphs of heaven carried away the poisons Surya's heat dissolved.

One afternoon, Aditi, that heavenly cow, vessel of all, spoke to Prajapati Visvakarmen at his smithy.

"Surya must marry," she said in her deep, slow voice.

"Hmmmm," agreed Prajapati. "Are you thinking what I'm thinking?"

And she was, for who better to marry this astounding red man than Sanjna, Bright Image, Prajapati's very own daughter?

Surya exulted when his mother told him the plan. He paced and questioned her exuberantly before he parked his chariot and rushed into the womb of the earth to clothe himself in his finest mantle.

Sanjna, however, felt afraid. At first, she acknowledged that Surya was lovely, his power beneficent, and his generosity legion. She even admitted she'd watched him in the evenings when the edges of his robe rippled on the path to his stables.

"Then, my daughter! It is settled!" Prajapati beamed.

"But, Father," she said, "I know I am called Bright Image, but even I need the shadows and the shade. Married to this Surya, I will never rest!"

"Hmmmmm," mused Prajapati, lacing his hands over his belly. "He will, in some ways, be a difficult husband. Mmmmm. If you are right, my precious, what can we do?"

"I am right, Papa," said Sanjna. "And I can't marry him! I just want to stay here with you!"

"My golden bell," said her papa, "if we can think of a way for you to rest, will you please your father and marry Aditi's child?"

Sanjna threw her arms around her papa and buried her face in his chest. Her shoulders shook and Prajapati Visvakarmen rocked her, clucking and humming.

"Yes, Papa," came finally her muffled voice. She drew back and looked at his face.

"That's my girl," said Prajapati, and he kissed her. "And I *will* think of something."

For days, Prajapati Visvakarmen ate, thought, and slept. Then suddenly, after a dessert of succulent cream pudding covered with coriander seeds and a warm red sauce, Prajapati Visvakarmen knew what to do. He called for his golden Sanjna and bade her sit for him while he modeled out of silver and iron a twin for her, alike to the lashes of her eyes.

"Papa, what are you doing?" asked Sanjna.

"Look, my darling, look," said Prajapati, and he breathed his blue breath into the second young woman.

Her lids fluttered and she woke as if from sleep. The twins, one shining, the other dark, gazed in shy wonder at each other.

Prajapati Visvakarmen placed their hands in each other's. "You are sisters!" he boomed. "Both my daughters. You, my Sanjna, my Bright Image, meet Shaya, my Shade."

"But, Papa . . . " began Sanjna.

Shaya, too, looked at him questioningly.

"Once each month, my Sanjna, when you must rest away from all brightness, you can go away into the shadows, and Shaya . . . you can stay with Surya and take your sister's place."

And so it was decided. Bright Image, with her sister, Shade, now had a way to rest, and the wedding could proceed.

Aditi sent her milky store so that the bride's thighs might shine, that sap might fill her feet with dance and loose her hair. The sages, serpents, and nymphs of heaven used a hundred-toothed comb to oil her locks. They dressed her in a red sari and golden veil. Every herb on earth sent up its fragrance for her perfume.

Prajapati Visvakarmen, that lord of life, bestower of luck, keeper of the seven tools, drew from himself the gold from which he made their marriage bed. Onto it he rolled the softest clouds, that they might waken from that couch laughing and reveling in each other.

Every flower on earth attended the ceremony. The constellations raised the canopy of heaven, then disappeared like thieves when Sanjna and her Surya showed their faces. The sages, serpents, and nymphs of heaven spun that celestial couple like clay upon a potter's wheel. Their splendid arms entwined each other, and they rose up like a ship with a hundred oars, flushing the morning with their joy.

Surya and Sanjna reigned in the north and the south, the east and the west, the highest and the lowest places. Sanjna, indeed, came to love her brilliant husband. And how wise she and her father had been! For when Sanjna could bear his dazzling no longer, she re-treated into the shadows and Shaya took her place. The two women birthed between them six children: Big Manu, Yama, Yami, Saturn, Little Manu, and Tapati. So alike were Sanjna and Shaya in voice, humor, and touch that Surya the Sun did not guess that he really had married two women.

But Yama, Sanjna's favorite child, one day grew angry with Shaya.

"Maybe you're not my mama!" he yelled. "You never let me do what I want!"

He had been whining and bickering the day long. Shaya suddenly struck him, impatient with this boy, who was not truly her child.

Yama swung back his little foot and kicked her. "You're NOT my mama!" he sobbed and ran for comfort to his father.

"What happened, my darling?" Surya asked his wife.

And Shaya told him the whole story.

Surya was furious. He changed himself to a fire red horse and plunged away to look for Sanjna. He found her quiet in a red flowering forest bathing in a hot spring. Red petals floated in the pool. His fury melted when he saw her.

He shed his horse's coat and kissed her wet feet. "Sanjna, Sanjna," he whispered, "I want you! I don't want your sister!"

Sanjna patted his head and rolled her eyes heavenward for inspiration. The sages, serpents, and nymphs of heaven raised their eyebrows.

Sanjna sighed. "Alright. Let's try it, darling, without Shaya," she said. "Perhaps Papa will take care of the children so that I can rest. Let's see how it goes."

Within a month, however, despite Prajapati's helpful grandfatherliness, Sanjna stood weeping at her father's smithy. "He is just too much, Papa," she sniffled. "He's wonderful, and then it gets to the point when I just can't stand it. I need the shadows."

Prajapati had another idea. This time he took his seven tools and went straight to his son-in-law. He bade Surya lie down and then, carefully, he ground away from the shining red man a full eighth of his brilliance. He trimmed away golden light from every part of him, except for his feet, the extent of which he could not discern. Then Prajapati Visvakarmen, that celestial artisan, made from the trimmings weapons for the gods. A discus for Vishnu, a trident for Shiva, a lance for Kartikkeya, and a hundred times a hundred spears for their hosts—all from Surya's superfluous rays.

Then Surya and Prajapati Visvakarmen gathered the family: Sanjna and Shaya, all the children, the seven horse brothers, and Aditi, that heavenly cow, vessel of all. They sang the melody, and the sages and serpents and nymphs of heaven sang the harmony of the ages behind it.

To this day, all of us can bear the splendor of the fullness of the light only because it has been shaved for our defense and because there lives with us always our sister shadow who takes our place when we need to rest.

The Rope from Heaven

FROM THE LUHYA PEOPLE, KENYA

The girl in this subtle drama is the human counterpart to the Greek girl-goddess Persephone (see "Baubo's Dance"). In contrast to Persephone's trauma and triumph, this story models a quiet, contemplative maturation process. In most versions of the Greek myth, the goddess is forced against her will into the underworld. There she finally marries the lord of the underworld and becomes queen of that realm. She brings light each spring when she climbs up to earth's surface.

The unnamed Luhyan girl, on the other hand, meets the divine when she willingly grasps a great umbilicus that pulls her into the realm of the sky. There she meets the Great Mother and marries the Sun of the realm. After the passage of time has readied her, she drops back into earth's dark. Finally, the story offers an image of a ripening feminine and masculine union that lights up the world.

The peaceful concerns of a precolonial time are reflected in this story. Today, the Luhya, more than a tenth of Kenya's indigenous population, maintain their cultural identity in a postcolonial world. They live on the lush green lands of western Kenya adjoining Lake Victoria. From 1952 to 1961, this Bantu-speaking people, along with their sister tribes, initiated the Mau Mau rebellion against British rule. This first great modern liberation movement of Africa was an epic of sacrifice, cruelty, and courage.

Though the passions of Mau Mau are dim memories and the people of Kenya are increasingly prosperous, they face the problems of a population explosion, tribal conflict, environmental degradation, and AIDS.

The Rope from Heaven

ONE MORNING, BEFORE THE pounding had begun of the maize in the mortars, a girl, filled with resolve, sneaked away from her village. Never would she marry that man! No matter how many cattle he had. She would die first.

Early in the evening, miles into the thick forest, the girl stumbled and fell forward into a clearing. She moaned from the pain of the fall and from fear: now that she was free of her parents' coercion, she was also absolutely alone. What would become of her?

The girl rolled over and lay still. In the twilight and her misery she did not at first notice the rope. Finally, she saw it dangling directly above her, wobbling gently. To her astonishment, it appeared to be attached to nothing, to descend directly from the sky. What could this mean?

Heart pounding, the girl grasped the rope with one hand and pulled herself to her feet. The rope hung taut, firmly bearing her weight. She tentatively took hold of the rope with both hands.

Instantly, the girl was lifted into the heavens. For a dizzy moment, the dark bush spun beneath her, and then—thump!—she landed in pure daylight next to a heap of marrow-sucked bones at the edge of a strange village.

The girl felt her limbs. They were whole. The ground was solid when she stamped. Satisfied, but too frightened to be curious, she drew her legs into her chest and rocked, her back and scalp tense.

"Who are you?" asked a regal old woman, who appeared suddenly at the trash heap.

"I am from a faraway village," said the girl in a low voice, not looking directly at the woman.

"Beautiful child," said the woman, "you can stay with me. I am the mother of the Sun."

The girl could say nothing. Her anger at her parents lay heavy in her stomach, and the vision of everyone at home sitting together sharing corn cakes and yams, wondering where she had gone, bunched in her throat. Two unspilled tears stood in her eyes.

"Come," said the mother of the Sun.

The house of the Sun was stuffed with sweet potatoes, bananas, and beans. While the girl feasted, the mother told her again how beautiful she was. "My son is chief," she said. "He will want to marry you."

The girl stopped eating. Had she escaped a forced wedding, only to be trapped again? She cast her eyes down. "I cannot marry a chief," she said politely.

Thinking the girl merely modest, the mother encouraged her. "Wait in the garden, my child, to meet my son. But you must not be afraid or cry if something very red and bright appears before you."

The girl ate a fig in the garden. It was fat and soft and sweet in her mouth. Suddenly the place was as brilliant as lightning. The Sun had returned, and the girl lay down to cover her face.

The Sun was enchanted with the girl's smooth dark skin. He welcomed her immediately as his new bride. The girl said nothing and did not raise her face.

The next day, the Sun sent his chief servant, the Moon, to speak to the girl. The Moon told her of the Sun's warmth and kindness. He said how honored the Sun would be to take her into his family to be one of his wives. The girl looked down and said nothing.

For each of the next six weeks, the Sun sent a new servant to talk to the girl. Each servant told her how happy the other wives of the Sun were, how rich was this land of the Sun. The girl would not reply. She only ate, and worked, and thought, and dreamed. She watched the Sun from a distance whenever she could, and she grew to see that this strong red man was handsome beneath his brilliance.

But the girl was not yet ready to speak. Even when the Sun sent her something of all that grew in the land, she was silent.

Finally, in the seventh week, the Sun decided to give her his own rays. He took them to the girl himself along with a huge, smooth pot. The girl's heart was pounding. She took the Sun's rays and put them into the pot.

"I will marry you, Sun," said the girl in a soft voice.

In time, the girl, now a young woman, felt herself deeply tied to her husband, his wives, her mother-in-law, and her three new children. But although the young woman did not know it, the happiness forged in heaven was not matched below. For the Sun's rays, shut away in the giant pot, no longer shone on earth.

One day, the young woman found herself making plans to return to her family on earth. The Sun helped her by dropping another rope out of the sky, on which the woman and servants clung, laden with presents.

The girl's family was huddled by a fire when she arrived. They were amazed to see her, for they had given her up for dead long before. From her mode of travel, they saw immediately that theirs was not an ordinary daughter. So they sacrificed not an ordinary ox but one of perfect white. They poured a portion of its blood at their spirit-daughter's feet; they roasted the rich meat; and all the people, heavenly and earthly, ate their fill.

The woman rejoiced and talked endlessly with her family. "We would be completely happy, oh daughter," said her parents, "if only we had light as we did before you were lost."

But in three days, when the woman and her servants made ready to return to heaven, the rope caught them up so quickly that she had no time to say good-bye.

Full of happiness and grief, the woman rushed to the pot in which she had hidden away her husband's rays. She snatched off the lid, and brilliant light once again showered the earth below.

"They are joyful, I know, at the return of your light," the woman told her husband. "They have been so long in darkness."

The Sun took his wife's face in his hands. "Then I will send my servant to light the night sky, too."

And so it is to this very day that Moon serves not only the Sun but also the Earth.

How the Sun Came to Belong
to Every Village

FROM THE SNOHOMISH PEOPLE,
PUGET SOUND AREA, NORTH AMERICA

*This is another story of balance between inner and outer challenges.
Its moral is about sharing; its plot, like so many others in this collection,
gives us metaphorical permission to be as inactive as we really want to
be during the winter. Effectiveness during our solstices won't come of
building biceps. Instead, silent solitude sets us ready to see the faceless
guides and to hear the tiny voice of Mouse. The story's crucifixion imagery recalls Christianity, but it is presented not as a triumph over death.
Rather, it invokes the ancient mythic formula that requires a balance of
life with death.*

*Snohomish County in Washington State is named for the Salish-
speaking native people who once called it home. Though the Snohomish
established a treaty with the United States government for the land in
1855, Anglo-Americans continued constant homesteading. That and
rampant disease decimated the Snohomish community. Like other tribes
who had never been exposed to the organisms carried by domestic European animals, they had little resistance to even the common cold.*

*This story was taken from the tellings of Chief William Shelton,
born in 1870, whose Salish name, Whea-Kadim, means "one who seeks
answers." This leader struggled poignantly with inner and outer balance.
Though groomed by his family to be a great medicine man, Whea-Kadim
took a second education at the Tulalip Indian Mission School in Puget
Sound. At his funeral in 1938, loudspeakers had to be set up on the lawn
to accommodate the crowd. Scores of famous personalities from both
nations, Native American women in bright shawls next to Anglo women
in fur coats, came to pay their respects to this man, who had worked to
turn timber into income and to bridge two cultures by helping to revamp
reservation schools.*

How the Sun Came to Belong to Every Village

Aт тне веginning, а реople in a village near Puget Sound owned the sun. At the center of the village lived a powerful chief with his wife and small son, Beead. Chief Sound let the sun shine day and night, so that his people did not know darkness.

The people of other villages, however, coveted the light. "Why should this village and not another," they asked, "own the sun?"

The Chief of the Far West, brother-in-law of Chief Sound, took action. "We should have a contest," proposed Far West. "Whoever can shoot the sun with his first arrow should own the sun."

Chief Sound and warriors from miles around took the challenge. Again and again they took aim at the sun. But repeatedly, their arrows fell short. It was Chief Far West, alone of all who tried, whose arrow hit the mark. Now, according to the agreement, Far West and his village owned the sun.

The people of the village near Puget Sound were filled with dismay. Not only had Chief Sound lost his position of power but, worse, they were now trying to work in the dark with only the red flicker of many fires for light.

"We must prepare for a new contest," proclaimed Chief Sound.

A host of young braves fashioned huge bows and strengthened their muscles for them. With perfect arrows, they sharpened their aims. Chief Sound was certain that he and his marksmen would retrieve the sun.

He said good-bye to his wife and to Beead, his son.

"Father, I have practiced, too," said Beead. "Please let me go with you."

Chief Sound smiled. "Not now, my son," he said.

Beead watched longingly as the canoes filled with his father and the marksmen vanished into the night.

"Brother-in-law," said Chief Far West when Chief Sound's company had arrived. "I will be most generous with you. Instead of just one arrow, your men may shoot all their arrows at the sun. If any can hit it, the sun shall be yours again. But if not, you and your men must die."

Chief Sound hesitated. He looked at his warriors. How beautiful they looked standing once again in daylight! Then he covered his heart with his fist. "We agree to your challenge," he said.

One by one, each archer fired all his arrows. Not one touched the sun. Finally, Chief Sound, with steady hands, fit an arrow into position, drew his bow to its fullest, and let fly the shaft to the whitely shining target. But just before it found its mark, the arrow veered into gray clouds that had gathered at the edges of the sky. The chief tried a second and third time, then again and again, until he had loosed his last arrow.

Far West's face was sad. "I'm sorry you missed," he said. "For now I must follow through on our agreement." The gray clouds covered the sun while Far West's warriors obeyed his orders. Chief Sound and all his company were hung on poles at the center of the village. A wind blew the clouds away, and the hanging men were left to die in the heat.

Time passed back in the village near Puget Sound. Chief Sound and his warriors did not return. People knotted together by the fires to wait and talk. "They have been killed, they have been killed," the people said.

The elders counseled together. "We must win back the sun," they said, "and we must avenge our chief's death."

Once again, a group of strong, brave men trained vigorously for the new contest. They ran and jumped and lifted. They increased their endurance and spread the girths of their chests. Every day they moved their practice target farther away. Beead, older now, and without his father to prevent him, made ready to join them.

But his mother shook her head. "This is not the way, my son," she said.

"Mother, I am chief now in my father's place," said Beead. "I must go."

"You must go, yes, but building your muscles is not the way," said his mother.

Beead looked at her wonderingly.

"You must go away by yourself, Beead. You must not eat or drink, and you must wait. The strength of the warrior comes when the body is weak."

Beead thought about his mother's instructions. He watched his comrades sweat and strain, exuberant in activity. Then, without understanding his own sense of certainty, he did as his mother had instructed. Without food, drink, or weapon, he walked far into the forest, beyond any marker he'd ever before explored. The moon curved twice into the sky before he came, hungry and thirsty, to the edge of a lake.

There he crouched, and then lay himself down, with a rock for a pillow, staring into the midnight waters.

Later, he told his children that he had seen unspeakable things. And a mouse had come to him, he said, and the mouse sang a chant that filled him, in his discomfort and fear, with strength. And then had come the *skalaletaad*. Never did Beead tell its shape or name, but somehow, when out of the depths this spirit had come, Beead's waiting had ended.

When he returned to the village, his face by the firelight was a boy's no longer. There was a kind of music in the way he moved, and he carried with him in a pouch next to his heart a mouse with whom he seemed able to talk.

Then with his braves, young Chief Beead dipped oars for the westward journey.

"Nephew," said Chief Far West, after they had arrived. "I am sorry you've come to risk your life and those of these fine men. Please return to your village. I am sure it is impossible for you to succeed, and if you fail, I must take your lives. This would cause great sorrow in my family."

Beead opened the pouch on his chest. "I understand the penalty, Uncle," he said. "I am not afraid to die."

Full of reluctance, Far West took his nephew and his party to the mark from which they would shoot. While he pleaded again with Beead not to try to win the sun, Mouse scuttled down Beead's leg and crept away into Far West's village.

There he found, shriveling on the poles, the bodies of the braves who had gone before. In the center hung the old chief.

Mouse hurried back and climbed to Beead's neck. Standing with his whiskers close to Beead's ear, Mouse whispered, "Your father hangs in the center of the village. Remember the song, Beead, remember."

Beead stroked Mouse. Then he stood a long time without moving. Chief Far West watched anxiously. Finally, Beead aimed at the sun. The arrow fell far short of its mark.

"Nephew!" said Far West. "Because you are my family, I will give you the chance, as I gave your father, to shoot all the arrows in your bag."

"Remember the song," squeaked Mouse.

Again, Beead stood very still. Then a music seemed to sing in the young chief. The bowstring pulled. The arrow surged. It struck the lower edge of the sun.

Chief Far West drew in his breath. "My nephew. I am proud of you," he said. "You and your people have won the sun. And I am now ready for my death."

"First we must take down your father," whispered Mouse.

Chief Beead and his men lifted the old chief's body from its stake. Sadly, Beead ordered his uncle hung in its place.

"It is time to sing the song aloud now, Beead," said Mouse. "I will direct the energy of the sun into your father's body."

The warriors built a giant drum and traded their weapons for drumsticks.

Now the music in Beead flooded from his throat. To the rhythm of the drum he chanted and tiny Mouse danced about the body of the old chief.

For hours Mouse dipped and turned and shuffled to the sounds of Beead's song. Then in the light of the sun, old Chief Sound opened his eyes. He tried to speak.

"Save your strength," said Mouse. "The time for words is later."

Beead and his men carried his father down to the first canoe, making him as comfortable as possible before starting the long journey home. Mouse stood at the edge of Far West's village and, with his paw, waved the sun to follow as they paddled.

Back in the village, the people began to fear that Beead had met the same fate as his father. Only his mother sat quietly, with a look of peace on her face.

Suddenly, a pale rose light misted into the heavens.

Slowly, pink deepened to orange. The people held one another. Then, yellow as the color of their joy, the sun burst into the sky.

The people cheered.

The canoes rounded the point. The people rushed to greet them.

A hush fell when the people saw their old chief.

Then, as if the villagers were water and Beead's mother a canoe, the crowd parted as she dreamwalked to greet the returning warriors. Her eyes were filled with tears.

The old couple wove their fingers together. The basket of the sky hummed blue.

Then old Chief Sound urged his son and the elders of the village to decide what should be done with the sun. "Why should any one village own the sun," he said, "and not another?"

The people decided to share the sun.

"It will move about the earth," they said. "When the sun is far away from a village, the night will be long; when it is close, the night will be short. But every village will have light at some time every day."

And so it has been ever since. Ho!

How the Cock Got His Crown

FROM THE MIAO-TZU PEOPLE, TRIBAL CHINA

*The sun-ray-like arrows of "How the Sun Came to Belong to Every
Village" figure also in this tribal Chinese story. So old that the mirror
is still an object of wonder, its plot is a charming concretization of the
psycho-spiritual truth "as above, so below." In our everyday lives, "as
above, so below" manifests most often as "as within, so without."* Synchronicity *is the word that describes that match of outer circumstance
to inner questions. We feel startled and grateful in the midst of a synchronicity. Synchronicity defies the Western notion of "mere coincidence"
and sends through us a rush of faith that there really is a pattern, even
if we cannot see it.*

Known today as the "National Minority Peoples," the Miao-tzu of
the modern southwestern Chinese provinces of Kuangsi, Kueichou, and
Yunnan are the descendants of the original peoples of China. Miao-tzu
roots are multitribal, each tribe with a distinctive region, costume, custom, and dialect. Like aboriginal peoples all over the world, their present-day existence as a culture, centered in the city of Wu Ch'ang on the
Yangtze River, is a tribute to their ability to survive with pride and grace
against invaders who would make them subject, destroy their culture,
and take their lands.

Legendary dynasties in the second century B.C.E. began the im-
mense undertaking of the colonization of the Miao-tzu. Because the
Miao-tzu refused to become Chinese subjects or to adopt Chinese customs, the Miao-tzu and the Chinese fought brutally for centuries. Racism,
usually an effective tool of subjugation, failed because the two groups
are racially indistinguishable.

Peoples who clash ultimately borrow from each other. They mesh
ideas, procedures, and language. The antipathies of the Miao-tzu and the

Chinese birthed tribal allegiances among the Miao-tzu, and the Chinese incorporated new ideas from the tribes.

I found this story in a form that mixed a Chinese emperor's wishes with the life of a Miao-tzu village. But the legend is Miao-tzu, so I have set it again in a purely village context that references tribal interaction rather than the interaction of tribe with dynasty.

How the Cock Got His Crown

ONCE, LONG AGO, WHEN the world had just begun, there were six suns shining in the sky instead of just one. One spring, the rains refused to come, and the six brother suns parched the earth with their great heat.

The farmers of every tribe watched in great dismay as the young green shoots they had sown with such effort baked brown in the white blaze.

The wise ones of a village in the west gathered with their chieftain. The chieftain's forehead was creased with worry. "Without food we shall surely die," he said.

From within the crowd an old man said, "The only help for it is to shoot the suns."

The chieftain's forehead relaxed. "That's it!" He clapped his hands. "We must gather from all the tribes the best archers. They must shoot down the suns!"

Strong archers from every tribe in the land traveled to the village in the west. Their clothes were of many colors, and they spoke different tongues. But all were ready to rid the sky of the dangerous brother suns.

Alas! Though their bows were hefty and their arrows swift, and six times six they tried, pouring sweat and grunting with exertion, not one arrow reached even halfway to the suns.

The archers looked at one another in great humility. In their many languages, they said, "The six sun brothers are too far away for our slender arrows."

People drooped sadly in the terrible broil. "How can we save ourselves?" they wondered.

Then suddenly, a sharp-eyed warrior from a faraway tribe, Howee, had an idea. Using his hands so that he could speak to all the people, he beckoned them to the edge of a pool of still water. There, moving ever so slightly on its surface, were reflected the six balls of blinding white. Howee pointed up with one hand to the heavenly suns and down with the other to the mirrored suns. Then, smiling hugely, he drew his hands together.

Ah! Howee seemed to be saying that the suns, in sky and water, were the same!

Howee drew his bow. But instead of shooting up into the sky, he aimed straight down into the pool. His first arrow pierced the first sun, which disappeared into the bottom of the pool. Ah!

He fired again, and the second sun disappeared, then the third, and the fourth, and the fifth sun. The people whooped. Howee was shooting down the suns!

When the sixth sun saw what had happened to his brothers, he fled over the hill. The people fell at once into an exhausted sleep. They planned to wake the next day to sow again their crops.

But alas! There was no next day! For the sixth sun, frightened and angry, had hidden himself deep in a cave and refused to come out.

The night went on and on. The chieftain's forehead crinkled again with worry. The wise ones gathered. "The crops will no more grow in constant darkness than they did in too much light," said the chieftain.

"We must send someone to coax the sun from his hiding place," said the old man.

The people first sent the tiger to the sun's cave. The tiger roared and roared for the sun to come out. He batted with his paw at the cave's door. The sun was resolute. "Go away!" he shouted. "I won't come out!"

The people then thought that the lowing of the cow might lure the sun. The cow begged gently outside the cave's entrance. But the sun was still sulking. "I won't come out," he yelled again.

At last, the people sent a cock to crow outside the hiding place of the sun. The cock puffed up his feathers. He neither asked nor begged, but simply shouted exuberantly. The sun was enchanted. "What a lovely sound," he said, and peeked out to see who could be making such music.

The cock, just as pleased with his own music, strutted and crowed again and again. The sun liked Cock's sounds so much that he came all the way out of his cave. Sun and Cock bowed to each other and Sun gave Cock a present of a little red crown.

Cock wears his red crown to this very day whenever he summons the sun. And, even if the sun is slow in the cold time, remembering with sorrow the deaths of his brothers, he never fails to greet his feathered friend, nor to light the day for the farmers who are growing their crops for the people to eat.

Sonwari and the Golden Earring

FROM THE THORIA, TRIBAL INDIA

This homely drama, from the Thoria tribe in the Kerba Koraput District of India, touches on the very loneliness of human existence. In it, the earring, hooked in the ear and lying close to the throat, symbolizes the abandoned, ignored, and unspoken stories of our lives. The relationships that witness and hold those stories have the power to light up the world.

The Thoria are Orissan tribal peoples. Orissa is a general name for a group of tribal peoples who actually have many different dialects and traditions (similar to the way Inuit *or* Eskimo *refers collectively to the various far North American tribal peoples). In general, the Orissa are farmers whose chief recreation is the dance; their social organization is patrilineal. Their myths and those of their Hindu neighbors have cross-fertilized each other. In the voice of the Orissan storyteller, this story is short and simple, almost taciturn, with no particular moral. So strongly communal is Orissan village life that the storyteller, like other individual personalities, makes no effort to stand out.*

Sonwari and the Golden Earring

Tᴴᴇ ᴠɪʟʟᴀɢᴇ, ɪɴ ᴛʜᴏsᴇ ᴅᴀʏs, was lit only by fire and the web of stars in the always-dark sky. There was as yet no sun, and the beautiful Sonwari still had both her astounding golden earrings.

Sonwari gasped with pleasure when she opened the wooden box in which they lay, a dowry gift from her mother and father. By flame light, she could see tiny worlds inside their spangled, wobbling pieces. She hung them in her velvet-clefted lobes, next to her full lips. Tilting coyly beside the innocence of her face, they hinted at her future knowing. They so hauntingly framed the bloom of her loveliness that people thought of aging when they looked at her, as they might think of clumsiness before a dancer in flight.

Sonwari was about to be married but had not yet met her new husband. The endless dusk obscured the vibrant yellow of her sari as she traveled to her new home. In rhythm with the plod of the cow beneath her, she pictured herself in a sprawling house with strangers all around her. Determination rose in her like a cud. She would make a place of respect for herself in this new life as her mother had once done.

As she pictured her mother's face wordlessly sending her good-bye, tears sprang to her eyes. She bit her lip and felt the tiny weights of her earrings swing delicately against her neck. She fingered them and was comforted.

After the wedding, the new family wrapped her so quickly in their foreign ways that not even her struggle showed. Like a fly in a web, she was bound to these new relations and to the stranger who was her husband. He came to her at sleeping times with a cape of maleness around him. She stroked him like a cat, wondering at his litheness, his neediness, his sudden inattention to her. She did not object to him; she was wistful. She wished she could tell him her won-derings, instead of just showing him her serene smile.

After every sleep, Sonwari took the earrings from their box. By candlelight, she could see in their intricacies the faces of her sisters and brothers left at home. She could see her mother's hands on the edges of the serving bowl, and her father's fist slap his palm as he laughed.

"Sonwari!" A call to work would interrupt her reverie. Quickly, as if she were taking her old family with her, she would slide the slim golden hooks, warmed by her touch, into her lobes.

Sonwari's father-in-law was an old man with a pocked face and the thinness of age in his eyelids and fingers. Fragile, having outlived his wife, his energy showed only in his stories, which seemed feeble to listeners who hoped for tales of heroics. But for Sonwari, his tales un-folded like food wrapped for safekeeping on a journey. He told stories of worlds that didn't show. He told of himself as a boy, longing for freedom during the night he had to guard the birds made drunk with tenderizing wine. He told of the sudden stab of fondness in his sol-dier's heart for the faces of his enemies. He told of his longing for the children who had grown. He told of touching the swollen water vats as if they were the bellies of women with children inside them.

The old man and the beautiful girl were drawn to each other. He, too, was a fly in a web, no longer the patriarch. He heard poorly and saw browns and grays where reds and blues had been. When he talked to Sonwari, he would roll tenderly the edges of her sari or hold for a moment on his fingertips the small heaviness of her earrings. Sometimes they would sit by the fire without talk, her head resting on his knee, one earring quiet against his blanketed leg, the other like a jewel near her throat.

One day Sonwari went to the well. As she uncoiled the rope into its depths, in the circle of fires in the village square, a fork-tailed kite with a hooked beak and long pointed wings swooped out of the night and ripped from her lobe one of the golden earrings.

Sonwari cried out. The rope slithered out of her palms, full pail emptying into the depths, as her hands flew to her ear and came away bloody. The bird sailed triumphant into the stars only to be caught, jagged in the prism of her tears, in their sparkling web. As the bird flailed to burst free, the earring tumbled from his giant claw and hooked on a strand of the web. There it hung, glinting gold among the silvery white of the stars.

Sobbing, Sonwari hauled the bucket up from the well's black hole and poured its contents into her jug. She stumbled home, unable to adjust her mask of calm other than to smear the back of her hand beneath her nose and press it against her teeth.

She set down the water jug and shakily took the remaining earring from her other ear. She took it to her father-in-law, who sat as usual near the fire, wrapped in a blanket in his basket chair. She knelt at his feet and cried and talked. He pulled her against his knees and stroked her hair.

The old man laid her earring in his papery palm, and squinted at it in the firelight. "You say he's stuck, the kite bird?" he mused.

Sonwari nodded.

"Little Sonwari," he said, "I tell you all the time what has happened already, no?"

Sonwari gulped and snuggled against those softly covered, bony knees. She tilted her head to look into his kind face. The light flickered.

"But not now, little Sonwari. I tell you now what *will* happen. That kite bird is stuck in the star web that the great spider spins across the sky." Her father-in-law chuckled. "He's like a fly up there. He can't get away. But your poor earring is growing bigger and bigger. So big, Sonwari, it will light up the world. Your earring is going to be the sun."

Even as he spoke, a strong shaft of light cut through the smoke hole across the pair of them, running a stripe of bright yellow across Sonwari's silk sari. Sonwari rose to her knees and searched the old man's face. In this light she could see the tiny lines connecting the pockmarks there.

"You see, Sonwari? I am right! Go. Look outside."

Sonwari ran from his side, ducking beneath the doorway and into the air. The sky outside was mauve, not black, bluing at the edges, and high above glistered a spangled, round, golden globe. By the time she'd returned from inside holding her father-in-law by his arm, the globe had bared itself so boldly that the sky was singing blue and the two of them could no longer look at the blaze.

The Sun Cow and the Thief

FROM THE KUTTIA KOND, TRIBAL INDIA

*This simple Orissan story from the Kuttia Kond of the Indian Koraput
District echoes the plot of the more complex Snohomish "How the Sun
Came to Belong to Every Village." Both stories are melancholic and
hopeful; told in modern voice, they are tales of the individual and the
collective.*

*The sun as a black cow is a fascinating image. But neither the idea
of the sun as a cow nor the paradoxical image of a dark light-giver are
as rare as we might think. Hindu tellers, neighbors to the tribal Orissa,
identified their sun Indra as a cow. Surya the Sun (see "Surya the Sun's
Marriage to Bright and Shadow") was born from the heavenly cow
Aditi. Go, the Hindi word for cow, also means "ray of dawn" or "ray of
spiritual illumination." In "Ra and Hathor," the Egyptian cow Hathor
is the source of Sun's light.*

*The Slavs (see "Solntse, the Girl at the End of the World") some-
times personified Fate as a slim, black woman with the legs of a cow,
long, teatlike breasts, and the eyes of a snake. The present-day altar of
Allat, the pre-Islamic Arabic goddess of light—possibly Sun herself—is
a black stone. Medieval alchemists spoke of* spiritus niger, *or the "dark
spirit," as the part of a deity swallowed up in his own creation, or as
the dark mystery of a deity's ability to transform to original luminosity.*

The Sun Cow and the Thief

Back at the beginning, the village was like a lovely box with many sides. A lonely man stood on the outside looking in. Through the cracks, he could see brightly colored crisscross lines everywhere. People walked to and fro along the lines, painting shimmering colors as they went. The man saw an order so neat and easy it seemed he should have been able to slide right in, the very blood in his body singing. But something was wrong with him, with the way things were. He could not get in. It was as if the village had no doors. Only windows. And the windows could never be broken. He could only look, never touch. He would always be on the outside, looking in.

Round the edges of the box, the sun cow walked. Round and round its perfect sides she walked, milking out her light in the day, filling the village box with color and warmth. At night, she chewed her cud, her black sides giving quiet warmth but no light.

The man stood between the sun cow and the village. The only warmth that the man could touch was the sun cow herself. Whenever those inside the village looked out, they saw only their sun cow, that lovely black heat, that night-chewer, that day-maker. They smacked their lips with the cream of it. They did not say, "Look at that nice man standing outside looking in! How silly that he stands alone at the edge when we could simply make a place for him in our lovely design of shapes and colors. Come, sir, you are welcome." They didn't say that; they didn't even see him.

And so the man waited for the sun cow every day, waited for her to pass him by, her big eyes soft like kind hands, her muzzle velvet and hot, and her flanks dark-scented. He felt the sun-honey-milk pouring out of her udder by some mysterious pressure. And he felt the pressure of his own sadness grow inside him.

All at once, one day, he decided to take the sun cow for himself. When all the pretty village people could not have her anymore, then, finally, everything might be fair.

So he waited for her, not even bothering to hide. The village people could not see him, after all, and she had walked sweetly near him, nonchalant, every day of his life. The day he stole the sun cow, he simply tossed a noose over her head and pulled her away. Away over the edge of the world. Away from the box. Away from all the can't-get-in. Away alone to the edge.

The lights and colors in the village plunged into darkness. Without the sun cow's milk there was only night. The people could not see. Babies cried, unfound and unfed by their mothers. No one knew when to wake up, when to work. All the order lay in shards, poking up from the endless dark like broken pottery in a just-plowed field. The tidy lines were lumped and smudged, the colors disappeared. Where had their sun cow gone? What had become of her? They waited in sorrow and fear.

The thief was having his own problems. At the beginning he luxuriated in the warmth of the sun cow's flanks, in her rhythmical grassy breath. But because she would not let him milk her, it was night for him, too. Now, away from her circling walk around the little box world, away from her habits, no light came from her udder. No one else had her, but now he didn't have her either.

When the thief, in desperation, tried to set beneath her a pail and to squeeze her teats, she kicked the pail away with such certain force that he feared that she would kick him, too, should he persist. She was only trying to save his life, of course, for just think what would happen to a single person who tried to milk the sun!

The thief held his head in his hands. For ever so long he sat, hoping for her light again, longing for a sign that he might milk her. Finally, he knew he could not keep her anymore. He leaned against her solid side for a good-bye, for a final giving-in to going back to the endless looking in and never having. Then he slipped the noose from its stake and from over her head and set the sun cow free.

But she did not return to her circling walk around the village. Instead she leapt up, high, joyously high, up over the moon. And now she walks not just around one village but in a vast sky circle around all the villages, around the circle of the whole world, so that no one now need simply look in without being part, without being seen. Everywhere there are intersections, connections, crisscross lines, shapes that can be walked in and about, shivering and shining with color. Everywhere there is light.

How Marsh Wren Shot Out the Sun

FROM THE MIWOK, NORTH AMERICA

The sun disappears in this story, too, because someone has been left out of the group. But like Howee in "How the Cock Got His Crown," Marsh Wren does his deed with an arrow. In both stories, a bird touched with red is responsible for Sun's return.

The Olamentko Indians of Bodega Bay, California, were one of the Miwok tribes, who made their homes for thousands of years on the north coast of California and the lower slopes and foothills of the Sierra Nevada mountains. The Miwok vanished at the turn of the twentieth century, driven out by white settlers. Anthropologists and mythologists, aware that a culture whose simplicity belied its richness was dying before their eyes, recorded the stories and memories of the few Miwok still alive. Today, on protected sites interpreted by museum curators, you can visit Miwok ghost villages set among the native nutritional and medicinal plants that this people knew so much about.

Stationary, not nomadic, many-tribed and many-languaged, the Miwok tribes shared a common understanding of the mythological origins and workings of the world and spun charming local variations on those themes. All Miwok peoples, for example, told of the exploits, adventures, and personalities of the First Creature-people, who finally transformed themselves into the animals and objects of the world—trees, rocks, cougar, stars, hail, rain. All told of Coyote-man, whose magic was almost always for the good. The Miwok said humans were created out of feathers, sticks, and clay.

The Hoo-koo-e-ko tribe of Tomales Bay told of First Person He-koo-las, who became Sun Woman, owing her brilliance to a coat of shining abalone shells. The last surviving member of the Olamentko tribe of Bodega Bay, north of San Francisco, told a brief, unsentimental version of this story of Tule-Wren (today called the Long-billed Marsh Wren) and Hummingbird. The story was published in 1910.

How Marsh Wren Shot Out the Sun

THE FIRST PEOPLE LIVED ON top of the great canopy of the sky. The sky had four holes in it, one in the East, another in the South, one in the West, and another in the North. The sky holes opened and closed rapidly all the time.

Just before Earth People were created, First People used their magic to change themselves into all the creatures, plants, and things of the world. Thus the Earth People had oak trees, and flat stones on which to grind the acorns of the oaks into meal. Thus the Earth People had reeds for houses and baskets. The Earth People learned from the sun how to shoot arrows like rays. They learned to live together as cooperatively as minnows swim and as cozily as mice nest.

But Cha-ka, the Marsh Wren, was an orphan boy. No one liked him. He had to go begging for food. "Cut-cut-turrrrrrr-ur!" he would whine in his reedy, gurgling voice. "More snails, more worms, more leeches, pleeeeease!"

The people gave Cha-ka food. Sometimes the people even gave him a crayfish to eat. But they always made Cha-ka feel like an outsider. So Cha-ka stayed under cover of bulrush and sedge grass, only appearing at dawn and dusk to ask again for more.

Cha-ka grew more ashamed, and the people grew stingier. "Get your own food, Cha-ka," they said. "We work hard. Why don't you? It's not our job to feed you, even if you are just a kid."

Marsh Wren's eyes filled with tears of anger. The white stripes over his eyebrows quivered. "If you don't feed me," he yelled, "I will shoot out the sun!"

Everyone laughed. "Yeah, right, Cha-ka. Go right ahead."

"I will!" rattled Marsh Wren.

"Do it," said the people, clearly not believing him. They turned away.

Marsh Wren did shoot out the sun with an arrow as sharp as his beak. As though it had been a bladder filled with light, the sun popped and all the light disappeared. The whole world became dark. No sun, no moon, no stars, no fire—everything was dark. The dark seemed to last for years. No one could find food because no one could see. Everyone was starving.

All this time, O-ye, the Coyote-man, was thinking about how he could get the sun and the light back again. At length he saw something way up in the eastern sky through the hole that opened and closed as fast as Woodpecker rapped on a dead tree trunk. "I think I see light!" said O-ye to himself. He squinted his eyes. Now there was no doubt. "Yes!" he exulted.

But a moment later, O-ye's tail dropped. "Now how am I going to go all the way up there to get that light?" he asked himself.

Glumly, O-ye began to pick his way through a tangle of old blackberry vines that led to his tiny stash of acorn mush. "Ouch! ooooo-Ouch!" he yelped as the thorns scratched at his nose and his soft footpads. O-ye remembered the good old days when this path had been blanketed with wet, curling ferns. The sun's beautiful light had slanted through the limbs of the gnarled live oaks, which were now too dark to see. "Oh cripes," muttered O-ye. "Drat and cripes."

"Drat and cripes, yourself," answered a high-pitched voice, followed by a "vrrrrrp."

"Huh? What? Who's there?" said Coyote-man. He heard another "vrrrrrp" sound and said, "Oh, hey! Hummingbird! How's it going, Koo-loo-pe?" Coyote-man was glad to have someone to talk to.

"Vrrrrp. Same old thing, Coyote-man. Same old thing. You know that," said Hummingbird. "If we just had some light . . . "

"Yeah," O-ye agreed automatically. Then near his eyes he felt the tiny wind stirred by Koo-loo-pe's wings. Suddenly he could picture his cinnamon, purple, and green-colored little friend, wings vibrating like twin haloes. He remembered him darting through the air faster than a fish flits through shallow water. "Hey! Hummingbird! I've got this great idea!"

"Vrrrrrrrp?"

"Koo-loo-pe!" sputtered O-ye. "Guess what I just saw? Just now? Light, Koo-loo-pe, light! I saw light way up high in the sky— way too high for me to get—but you, Hummingbird—you could get it in a second."

"You saw light, Coyote-man?" The little voice was incredulous. "Where?"

"Up high, Hummingbird! Really! Go look. I know you can bring it back for us."

The tiny wind of Koo-loo-pe's wings stopped for a moment. O-ye could imagine his friend hesitating. Then he heard a reassuring "vrrrrrrrrrrrrrrp!" and he just knew Hummingbird was splitting the black air in a steep climb to the top of the sky.

"It would be crrrrrrrrazy not to try!" shouted Koo-loo-pe, but he was already too far away for Coyote-man to hear.

Up, up, up rushed Koo-loo-pe, until he, too, could see the dab of light blinking inside the mouth of the hole in the eastern sky. Nearer and nearer he sped, until, heart beating wildly with his own daring, he shot through the hole and tore off a piece of the blazing orange light on the other side.

"Vrrrrrrrrp! I got it!" yelled Koo-loo-pe. He tucked the fire under his chin and hung for a moment in the air, surveying the amazing flood of light. But suddenly a sound of giant wings flapping filled the space around him. In a burst of fear, without even looking to see what or who might be following him, he raced back toward the hole in the sky.

Through it he flung the fire, and then he swooped after it. All around him, the air turned pink and blue. The fire he'd carried swelled round as a puffball and sent arrows of light down to the earth below. People gathered on the shores of the bay, cheering, and Coyote-man whooped and howled. Even Cha-ka, the Marsh Wren, muttered with pleasure. "Cut-cut-turrr!" he said.

Koo-loo-pe, now glitteringly graceful in the light of a new sun, sped toward his nest. His feathers shone as they had in the old days: metallic bronze-green, jewel-like purple, and rich golden cinnamon. But when Koo-loo-pe modestly lifted his head to acknowledge the happiness of everyone below, the feathers on his throat against which he had carried the light were tinged a new brilliant scarlet, the color of sunfire. And so Hummingbird is marked to this very day.

The Marriage of Sun King
and Silver Moon

FROM THAILAND

*The Shan, or Thai, people have long occupied the lands near the Red
and Yangtse Rivers in the east and north and the upper Mekong Valley
in the west. They call their country* Muang Thai, *or "Land of the Free,"
honoring their hard-won victories against the Chinese, Tibetan, Por-
tuguese, Spanish, Dutch, French, English, and Japanese invaders.*

Sanuk *means "fun" in the Thai language, which has forty-four
consonants and thirty-two vowels. The hot, ancient courtship of the Sun
King and Vela Chow in this* sanuk *tale must have felt like an April noon
in modern Bangkok. The stars in this tale keep the balance between hot
and cool, day and night. They could be metaphors for the wisdom of
the body twinkling quietly in the dark world of the cells. Though we
are encouraged to ignore the hunches and urges of the body, meeting our
needs for food and water, rest and sleep, movement, beauty, touch, and
silence is like caring for a musical instrument. Only when the instrument
is carefully tended can the sounds of desire and understanding blend in
harmony.*

The Marriage of Sun King and Silver Moon

IN A CAVE BY THE GREAT Chao Phraya River, the Sun King once lay with his beloved so long that paradise on earth was lost. But that was before her name was Silver Moon, and before the Stars had made their bargain with Sun.

It happened long ago when Sun was young. Every day he trotted his mares and stallions across the sky, sometimes exuberantly urging them into canter. Sun King's own glittering, rippling warmth swelled the realm of the Earth King with tamarind, lime, and red banana. All of Earth King's people ate all the rice they wished, and no one was ever sick.

Every evening, Sun King set his steeds to rest in their shining stables. Inside his spiraled castle, he feasted on coconut soups fragrant with lemongrass. While Sun King rested, the Stars crowded into the night sky, visiting and holding council together above the peaceful sleepers below.

In this auspicious time the Earth King's principal wife birthed an astoundingly lovely little girl. Even before she arrived, the soothsayers called her Vela Chow, Beautiful Dawn. "She will turn the head of Sun," they said. "He will fall in love with her."

Even as a tiny child, Vela Chow was beloved of the people and the Stars. The people praised her soft, peachlike glow. Early each morning, the Stars cuddled their rosy little friend and told her stories.

"Horsies!" Vela Chow would crow when she heard Sun King's horses begin their gallop. Then, nuzzling inside the laps of her star friends, Vela Chow would peek in delight as Sun King's chariot broke into the sky.

Beautiful Dawn was a young woman when Sun King first noticed her.

One morning, Vela Chow was bathing in the Chao Phraya River. Cradled in its limpid water, she rolled on her back, her face turned up to the dome of the sky. Her eyes were dreamy, with her full lips parted just enough to show her pearly teeth.

Startled, Sun King reined in his horses. Heart pounding, he stared at the exquisite young swimmer below.

Unnerved by his gaze, Vela Chow sprang to her feet in a shower of droplets made diamond by Sun's radiance.

Both Sun King and Beautiful Dawn cast down their eyes in a rush of shyness and then began to speak at once. The people looked at one another when they heard their laughter. "Vela Chow has turned his head," they said. "They're going to fall in love with each other."

It was true. Vela Chow and Sun King soon had eyes, ears, lips, and voices only for each other. It seemed to Beautiful Dawn that she could never memorize his stunning face; Sun seemed never to tire of her eyes and her stories.

Finally, Sun King quit altogether going home to his palace in the evenings. He tied his horses near a cave at the bank of the Chao Phraya. There, Sun King strung garlands for Vela Chow's neck, waist, wrists, and ankles. He played with her long fingers while they talked and joked and listened to each other.

But the people sweltered in Sun's constant presence. It was too hot to work. The people began to long for the easy night. The Stars were amused and tolerant at first; they loved their Vela Chow. But they grew annoyed at the broken rhythm of their rule and they missed the silent depth of the dark.

It was a relief to everyone when Vela Chow and her Sun King hid in the cave to melt into each other's arms.

A honey of darkness dropped over the world. The people sank into sleep. The Stars wasted no time. They sped to Earth, untethered Sun's horses and chariot, and hid them away. Chortling with their own cleverness, they posted themselves to watch in the sky.

The day had seemed unending before. Now it was the night that did not lift. The birds stopped singing. A dread settled over the people, and they grieved the blessed balance of the light and the dark.

When the lovers finally emerged from their cave, Sun King flared with anxiety when he could not find his horses and chariot.

Vela Chow did not understand. "Just stay here with me, my darling," she pleaded.

"But I've got to light the world," said Sun. "I've got to find my horses."

Reluctantly, but not wishing to separate from him even in his worry, Beautiful Dawn climbed Mount Inthanon with Sun. Inside every rocky pocket they searched, but to no avail.

Sun King kissed Vela Chow distractedly and gestured to the heights of heaven. "I must look for them at my palace," said Sun. "Come, take my hand, and we'll jump there."

Vela Chow clung to her Sun. "I can't do it," she whispered. She wept tears of silver, and Sun mopped them with his thumbs. His own eyes spilled out tears of gold, and the two kissed each other's faces again and again.

"I will come for you when I find my chariot," promised Sun, and Vela Chow watched in misery and wonder as he plunged upward into the sky.

Sun flung open the door of his palace. "Where are my horses?" he yelled. "Where is my chariot?" He charged into his throne room.

There, tapping their feet and sucking their teeth, waited the Stars.

"Where are they?" demanded Sun.

"We have them safe and ready for you," said the Stars.

"Where?" shouted Sun.

"You shall have your horses and chariot and again be King of the Day," said the Stars. "But you shall have them if, and only if, you agree never again to shine in the night."

"I agree," said Sun. "Now where are my horses?"

"That is not all," said the Stars. "You have your work, Sun. It is your task to light each day. Now that she is grown, Vela Chow has her work, too. From now on her name will be Silver Moon, and she shall be Queen of the Night. You may come to her only when she is not shining."

"Of course I will light the day," said Sun. "But I will visit my queen whenever I choose."

The Stars raised their eyebrows and shook their heads. "Only when she is not shining," they repeated.

Sun looked at the Stars, who were pressed into his throne room and spilling out its windows and doors. He saw that it was useless to argue with so many of them. He swallowed.

"Alright," said Sun, "I agree."

And so the Sun King and Silver Moon with her court of Stars took their balanced places in the sky. And the people on the earth below made festivals and fireworks and played flutes and gongs and drums.

And to this very day, Sun almost always keeps his bargain with the Stars. Never does he shine at night; almost always he shines during the day. He waits to visit Moon on the other side of the sky until she closets her silvery robes and veils herself in soft black for him. Only during the time that people call the "eclipse" does Sun make his way, filled with unbearable longing, across the heavens to be with his Moon when she is shining.

The Light Keeper's Box

FROM THE WARAO PEOPLE, VENEZUELA

On March 31, 1880, thousands of people gathered in Wabash, Indiana, the first American municipality to be lit by electric lights. Bands played, guns fired salutes, and then the lights sprang to life. A hush fell over the crowd. Some people groaned and fell to their knees.

Such a wonderful vigil as this seems almost as foreign to us over a neon-century later as daylight itself must have seemed to the villagers in this story, which comes from the only purely aboriginal people left in Venezuela.

Spanish explorer Alonso de Ojeda named the country Venezuela— "little Venice"—after the tree houses built by the Warao of the equatorial Orinoco River delta. Still animists in 1850 despite more than three centuries of Spanish colonization, the Warao preserve to this day a remnant of gift instead of commodity culture: a socioeconomic set that continually circulates—like blood through a body—offerings from plants, animals, and people. In gift culture, giving away parts of the self is the process that forms community. Gift culture moistens the spirits of all beings with generosity and cooperation.

In a world teeming with spirits, even a simple box woven of itiriti leaves is alive with dreams and visions. The plant itself, teach the Warao, is a gift from the body of a primordial ancestor. This story is full of gifts. The light keeper's generosity moves toward emptiness and darkness. The gift continues to move: the light is given away to the whole village. Turtle is finally the symbol of the slow, sweet gift of friendship.

Meister Eckhart, the thirteenth-century German mystic, said, "Let us borrow empty vessels." The itiriti box could be such a vessel, representing that strange truth that new life comes to those who surrender.

The Light Keeper's Box

A T T H E B E G I N N I N G , T H E world by the Orinoco River was indistinct because the people had only wooden torches to illu-minate their villages. By the flicker of their light, neither day nor night truly existed.

In the midst of one village lived a chief with two daughters. News came to the chief of a man somewhere who kept the light. The man called to his older daughter and said, "Go and see where this young light keeper is, and bring some light to me." Then he blew on her face so that the *hebus* of the bush, water, and sky might leave her safe.

The young woman, wearing her most lovely *mauritia* apron, packed herself a small sack, and left. Just outside the village she found many roads on which to travel. She didn't know which one to take.

The one she finally chose led her to the house of Deer. He greeted her with his soft eyes and his antlers like fuzzy tree branches above his smooth ears. She stayed with Deer a long time, laughing, talking, and loving with him.

When at last she returned to her father, however, she did not have the light.

The father decided to send his younger daughter. "Go and see where the young light keeper is, and bring some light to me." He blew on her face. "I will play my flute for you, too," he said.

The young woman combed out her hair and set off. She, too, came to the many roads and could not decide which one to take. But she heard the faint sound of her father's flute, and a feeling about the roads crept over her. They seemed to have faces, and she chose the one that seemed strong and old. Finally, after much walking, she came to the house of the light keeper.

The light keeper's face was as young as the road had seemed old. "I have come to meet you," she said, "and to get from you some light for my father."

"I have been waiting for you," the light keeper answered. "Now that you have arrived, come stay with me."

The young man took up a box, made of tightly woven *itiriti* leaves, that he had at his side. Carefully, so that the dreams inside would not spill out, he opened it. The light colored his sinewy arms brown and his teeth white. It poured a sheen over her black hair and dark eyes.

And so the young woman discovered light. After showing it to her, the young man closed the lid of the *itiriti* leaf box.

But every day, the light keeper opened the *itiriti* leaf box, so that he and the young woman could enjoy themselves in the light. They laughed and played and saw visions sweet as honey wine.

But it happened that one day the young woman remembered she had to return to her father and bring to him what he had sent her to find. The light keeper held the woman close. Then, as a present, he gave her the *itiriti* box filled with dreams and light. "I want you to take this with you," he said.

The young woman found her father asleep in his hammock. "Father," she whispered, "the *hebus* have left me safe, and I have brought you light."

The chief woke fully and welcomed her. She showed him the light trapped in the leaf box. He hung the box from one of the stilts that held up his house. Its dreams drifted out, and rays of the light touched the crinkled water of the Orinoco, the fan-shaped leaves of the *ite* palm, and the yellow-red fruits of the *merey*.

Word spread to all the neighboring villages that a family down the river had light. People traveled to see it for themselves. They arrived in their long, thin, purpleheart bark canoes, down this channel and that, boats and more boats, filled with people and more people.

Everyone packed themselves inside the house of the chief. They marveled at the light and at the new pictures that came while they slept. The man and his daughters fried fish after shimmering fish for their guests. Even their porch filled with people, until the slim stilts of the house could no longer hold the weight of so many. But since the light's clarity was so much more agreeable than the firelit darkness, no one left.

Finally, the chief could not stand so many people. "I am going to end this," he said. "We *all* want the light, so here it goes!"

With a wonderfully strong toss, he hurled the *itiriti* box and its light into the sky. The body of the light flew to the East and the box rolled to the West. The body of the light became the sun. And the box, tightly woven of leaves as it was, turned into the moon.

On one side was the sun, and on the other, the moon.

But because the chief's throw had been so powerful, the sun and the moon moved very rapidly. The day and the night were very short, with sunrise and sunset following quick upon each other.

The chief had an idea. "Bring me," he said to his younger daughter, "a little turtle."

The young woman brought, cupped in her hands, a little gray turtle. The father blew on the turtle and then waited until the sun was just overhead. "Sun! I'm giving you a present!" he called out. "Take this turtle to be your friend. She is yours. I give her to you. Wait for her!" Then he took up his flute.

The little turtle journeyed up to the sun, the sweet notes of the flute warbling beneath her. And because turtles do not hurry, Sun had to wait a long time for his gift. When Turtle finally reached him, Sun walked very slowly across the sky so that he might keep step with his new companion. Moon ambled across the sky so as not to interrupt the beginning of this new friendship.

And to this day, when Sun gets up in the morning, almost always he travels at Turtle's pace, so that the day lasts just long enough until the night comes to the world by the Orinoco River.

Sun Man and Grandfather Mantis

FROM THE SAN PEOPLE, KALAHARI DESERT

Here is a story that celebrates not just bodily balance *but bodily* indulgence. *The route to shining comes through the shenanigans of a hilarious trickster, I Kaggen, old Grandfather Mantis. Crabby, boastful, with a powerful sweet tooth, Mantis's thinking strings are much easier to hear after an unapologetic quest for luxury. And the children are the ones to finally send Sun Man up into the sky. Outside and inside, the children focus on what really matters.*

The San, a Bush People who live in the southern Kalahari Desert of southwestern Africa, fought fiercely for their land and their lives when, centuries ago, yellow- and black-skinned peoples from the north, and finally whites from across the sea, colonized southern Africa. Tortured beyond endurance, the Bush People finally made their home in the desert, where no one else wanted to live.

Some say the Bush People are the greatest storytellers of all. Wild, mystical, funny, these charming characters, made familiar to me by Jenny Seed's The Bushman's Dream, *inhabit a world made by the Early Race of Creature-people, whose spirits still watch over all (see introduction to "How Marsh Wren Shot Out the Sun"). A Bush person feels bound to birds, insects, water pans, and animals. San feet dance when springbok feet rustle; San faces smile for the blackness of the stripe on the face of the springbok.*

Sun Man and Grandfather Mantis

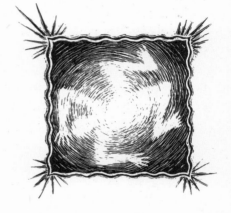

N O ONE BUT THE ANTELOPE knows exactly where Grandfather Mantis lives anymore. But everyone knows to thank Grandfather Mantis for Sun Man's living up high in the sky. Even before the people of the Early Race knew they were the People of the Dream, and before the Dream People were Altogether Creatures, Grandfather Mantis was old, and Sun Man was young and lived on the earth.

He rose early in the morning. He yawned and stretched out his graceful arms, spreading the fingers of his small hands. Out of his armpits streamed a great light for all the people. Grandfather Mantis rocked on his porch, soaking up Sun Man's warm, yellow light into his skinny old bones. Not so long before, the Ant People had attacked Grandfather Mantis and eaten him up. But Grandfather Mantis had used his magic to join up his bones again and to come back to life. He chuckled now to think of it and tapped the big old brown tooth in his head where all his power lay.

"Heh, heh, forgot to take my tooth, they did, Rock Rabbit," he said to his wife. "Forgot to take my tooth."

Rock Rabbit looked up from painting water designs on ostrich legs. "You're a lucky old man," she said.

"Heh! Heh! So you're a lucky old woman!" chortled Grandfather Mantis, and he tapped his tooth delightedly.

Sun Man's light shone down on Grandfather Mantis's porch, on Rock Rabbit, and on Old Sister Blue Crane, who was gathering melons and berries. Grandson Mongoose played a pebble game in a knot of other children, while his mother, Porcupine Daughter, stitched together the thongs of a sandal. Her husband, Kwammanga, the Spirit of the Rainbow, lay stretched in a hammock with his feet hanging down.

Sun Man's light shone, too, over the Lion People, who slung food bags over their right shoulders and quivers of poisoned arrows over their left. Silently they hunted the springbok, who jumps high in the air when surprised. In that distant beginning season, Sun Man's warm magic flowed over all the land. Whenever he raised his arms, it was day. Whenever he lowered them, it was night. The Bee People and the Elephant People and the Tic People loved the rhythm of Sun Man's light. Their faces crinkled with pleasure in his heat.

But inside the dreamtime, Sun Man grew old. His back grew stiff and his knee joints ached. He rose later and later each morning. He napped soon after breakfast and went to bed in the afternoon.

"What's going on here?" complained Grandfather Mantis. "I'm not getting heat anymore." Grandfather Mantis sent the Bird People to find out.

The Bird People returned, rumpled and solemn. Darkness was everywhere, even though it was supposed to be daytime. "Sun Man is getting old," they explained. "This shining all the time is getting too much for him."

"Well, I'm old," snapped Grandfather Mantis. "Doesn't stop me."

His wife raised her eyebrows but said nothing.

"I'm cold, Mama," said Mongoose, Porcupine's son.

Porcupine Daughter pulled Mongoose close. "Everything is broken!" she mourned to her husband, Kwammanga.

Everyone was listless and sad.

"We cannot live this way," said Sister Blue Crane worriedly. The children pressed around her thighs for warmth.

For a long time Grandfather Mantis said nothing more, except to complain about the cold and whine because his food was not hot.

Rock Rabbit shook her head. "Tji!" she said. "Complain, complain, complain. If you don't like it, Old Man, why don't you do something?"

Grandfather Mantis did not like to listen to his wife's scolding. He began to long for something sweet. "My body needs strength," said Grandfather Mantis, "so I can listen to my thinking strings when the wind blows."

He took off his sandal and threw it hard on the ground. The sandal turned into a dog. Grandfather Mantis sent the dog to fetch him a nest of honey.

The dog came back with just one piece of honeycomb.

"This is not enough," snorted Grandfather Mantis. "My thinking strings need much more honey than this." And he sent Mongoose away to fetch him the whole nest.

Mongoose took a long time to bring the honey to his grandfather. Mantis was irritable. "Why do you take so long?" he said.

Mongoose started to speak, but Rock Rabbit interrupted. "It's dark everywhere, Old Man," she said. "Of course the child takes long to find his way."

Grandfather Mantis sucked piece after piece of honeycomb. He swallowed slowly and smacked his lips. Suddenly, a wind outside blew through the little bush hut where everyone huddled. Mantis's wings trembled. "I can hear my thinking strings move!" he cried. The wind continued to blow, and Grandfather Mantis continued to tremble.

Rock Rabbit and Sister Blue Crane looked at each other significantly.

Finally, Grandfather Mantis called Mongoose and all the other children to him.

"Go to the place where Sun Man is sleeping," he told them. "Grasp him firmly and throw the old man into the air. His armpits will open and once again we can get warm all over."

The children did as Grandfather Mantis said. They crept up to Sun Man, making no more noise than the hunter following the springbok. They stood still and waited until their eyes could make out in the darkness just where to hold Sun Man.

The children put their hands under Sun Man. He felt hot all over. Together they lifted and then heaved Sun Man into the air. Over and over he tumbled. His arms and legs opened wide to keep his balance. Hot beautiful light poured from his armpits.

"Sun Man!" Mongoose shouted. "You must go up high in the sky. You must make heat and light for us, so we will no longer be cold and so the whole earth will have day!"

Sun Man heard. He let himself grow hot as fire and let his tumbling turn him round as a ball. That day, Sun Man became a bright circle of heat up high in the sky.

Grandfather Mantis was proud. He tapped his old brown tooth. "What man is equal to me? Who but I have the magic?" Thin legs shuffling in the dust and head nodding, he began a gay and boastful dance.

Rock Rabbit looked at Old Sister Blue Crane and shook her head. How could she scold her husband when everyone was warm again and there was light to eat and work and visit by?

All that first day with the new Sun Man high in the sky, the people rejoiced. They ate their fill of meat and drank the cleanest water. They put on their finest clothes because now everyone could see one another.

When the new Sun Man went away for the night, Porcupine Daughter smiled at Kwammanga. "Everything is put back together again," she said.

The Spirit of the Rainbow smiled back. "Now is the time for the stars," he said.

The Sun, the Stars, the Tower, and the Hammer

FROM THE BALTIC PEOPLES,
ANCIENT NORTHERN EUROPE

Jerome of Prague recorded in the early 1400s a Lithuanian tribal story of the sun's imprisonment by a powerful king in a tower. They worship the sun, he wrote, and venerate the large iron hammer, forged by the signs of the zodiac, that broke open her jail.

Present-day Latvians, Lithuanians, and Estonians—as well as the wholly assimilated Old Prussians—are the descendants of the Baltic peoples of ancient northern Europe. The Baltic girl-woman sun, Saule, inspired countless pieces of still-extant Baltic poetry and art. Called both Mate for "mother" and Meita for "daughter," Saule's imagery fills poem after psalmlike poem. She rides in a boat and chariot to a place in the invisible world where the dead continue to live, just as she herself shines through the night though we cannot see her. Baltic folklore—their stories, songs, and proverbs—is one of the richest in all of Europe, revealing the ancient reverence for a world of living forests, hills, trees, springs, stones, and mountain slopes.

For more than two thousand years preceding the Christian crusades of the eleventh century, the Balts had worshiped the elemental world. For another four hundred years, country folk preserved their faith despite the strict outlawing of their rites and music by Christian nobility.

To the seed of Saule's story, I have added both Kalvaitis, the Baltic celestial blacksmith, counterpart to the Greek Haephestus, and the plot device of Saule's not having cried before being locked in the tower.

The zodiac, which comes from the Greek for "living being," pictures the universe as a complete circuit or circle. Russian folklore preserves the sun as keeper of twelve kingdoms, with stars as her children. The twelve equal parts of the zodiac, each bearing the name of a constellation, correspond in astrology to the complexities of physical, psychological, and spiritual experience.

The Sun, the Stars, the Tower, and the Hammer

SAULE THE SUN SLIPS SILENTLY each day into the orchards of apples. There she loosens the silver brooches of her silky white shawl and hangs her scarlet belt on the oak at the center. The oak's leaves are silver, its gnarled branches copper, and its reaching roots iron. Saule dances in her silver shoes, red fern blossoms tucked in the twists of her braids. Her cheeks flame rosy as the apples as she sways and hops and rolls. Then, hair barely bound, blossoms littering the meadow, she rests, drinking up her liquid light from her round yellow jug.

Each evening, Saule journeys in her copper chariot away from the apple orchards, over the hills of silver, down to the edge of the sea. Into the waters she strides with her steeds, their hundred coats hot as fire but not sweating. Then she bathes them cool again, their golden reins hanging loose at their bridles. Finally, red crown glowing, she steps into her golden boat to sail beyond the hills of the souls to the center of the world. There she sleeps in her castle coiled about with the eons and the days.

All day long, Saule presses her lips against the bare skins of those who pray to her. All the dead return to Saule, mother of life, who before she was locked in the tower had never cried.

No one knows quite how it happened. Some say a cruel king built a tower and locked Saule inside. Some say it was a queen, vexed with Saule's heat and power. Some say Saule went herself, out of curiosity, and the wind slammed shut the door and whirled away the key. However it happened, the structure had neither window nor crack, and its bricks were formed of darkness, its single door a slab of night.

Everywhere, the people mourned. Their light had fled, the golden boat submerged, the yellow jug cracked, and the apples gone soft and gray, fallen from the murky branches.

Even Kalvaitis, the Smith of Heaven, noticed the dark. A hush had fallen on the world. Kalvaitis, shut away in his tool-filled chambers, raining down sparks of silver upon the waters as he worked, noticed the strange silence when he rested from his crafts.

Then he heard a noise swell from below. People were shouting to the stars. "Bring back our sun!" they begged, voices full of fear and sorrow. "Bring back Saule!"

The constellations—ram, bull, twins, crab, lion, winged lady, scales, scorpion, archer, goat, water-bearer, and fish—heard the peoples' cry. Protectively, they circled the world, talking and arguing about the best way to help. Finally, they hit upon a plan. They went to the Smith of Heaven.

"We've come, Kalvaitis," said Aries the Ram, "to help you make a Hammer."

"A hammer?" asked the Smith of Heaven. "I have plenty of hammers."

"This Hammer will be separate and different," said the Ram, "from any ever seen before. It is a Hammer to smash the tower that traps the Sun."

"Ah!" said Kalvaitis. "So she is trapped! I thought I noticed that she was not here. In a tower, you say?"

"Built from earth to heaven," bellowed Taurus the Bull. "And we've no time to waste: the fruits are rotting in the fields, and no one can see to pick them." A vein bulged in the Bull's neck. "I give your shoulders, Kalvaitis, extra strength for this forging."

The Gemini Twins gestured with their four hands. "You'll need special materials," they intoned. "Body and mind, mortality and immortality, all and nothing. We'll blow our wind through your bellows."

Kalvaitis shook his head. "I thank you," he said. "I want to do this, I do. But I . . . "

"But you have so many other things to do," smiled Cancer the Crab, feeling herself round and soft under her hard shell. "Kalvaitis, as a baby longs for mother's milk, may you long to make this Hammer."

Leo the Lion put a paw on Kalvaitis's heart. His mane bristled. "Kalvaitis, your Hammer will break Saule's tower in just three blows."

"But . . . " began Kalvaitis, "I need . . . "

"You need precision of timing," said Virgo, the Lady with Wings of Wheat and Corn. "I give you judgment and discipline strong as iron."

Libra the Scales spoke evenly. "The halves of you—above and below, side and side—will flow together. Your work will be one with your idea."

The Scorpion laughed. "The work is essential. No doubt about it," she said. "But sleep, too, Kalvaitis! You must also sleep. I give you that sweet, mysterious dark. Renew yourself for the forging of Saule's Hammer."

Kalvaitis bowed his head.

"I see you despairing of the responsibility," said Sagittarius the Archer. She stretched up to reach Kalvaitis, her muscles taut. She touched him. "Do not fear. I fill you with optimism."

"And I," said Capricorn the Goat, "fill you with just enough doubt to make you flexible. Plant your hooves, Kalvaitis—try again and then again!"

Aquarius, the long-haired boy with the Giant Urn, spoke next. "Here are the waters," he said, "to cool the Hammer."

Kalvaitis clenched and unclenched his fists. Slowly, he looked from one constellation to the other.

Pisces the Fish swayed gracefully. "We've given you our gifts, Kalvaitis," she said. "But you are the Smith. We all know your compassion and imagination. That's why we came to you."

Everyone waited quietly. Then said Aries the Ram, "We have spoken."

A great rummaging sound welled up as all the constellations— ram, bull, twins, crab, lion, winged lady, scales, scorpion, archer, goat, water-bearer, and fish—began to hum and shuffle. Kalvaitis closed his eyes. They circled around him, twinkling, touching him, and crooning him to sleep. The wheel of time turned itself backward and forward before Kalvaitis opened his eyes again and bent to his work. The stars hovered, winking at one another in satisfaction as they watched the Smith of Heaven wield intention, strength, tools, and skill.

Far away, Saule, locked in her tower, had been rocking, her face frozen. Suddenly, a strange water filled her eyes. The water spilled down her cheeks and a noise tore from her throat.

Kalvaitis merged air, metal, fire, and water.

Locked in the tower, Saule's tears came so freely that they washed hot around her feet. Swollen and exhausted though she was, tenderness and hope sparked within her.

Kalvaitis finished the Hammer. His shoulders had been strong; the winds of his bellows mighty. The Hammer was separate and different from any seen before.

Saule, in her tower, blind and deaf to the world without, felt her skin tingle with sudden expectation.

Kalvaitis swung the Hammer. One! Two! The constellations hummed. Three!

With a roar and a whipping crash the neck of the tower broke, and Saule the Sun burst from its shambles. She somersaulted. She soared.

The hillsides glinted again, tinting and elongating with color. The country folk flung open their doors and cavorted in the meadows.

Saule's hundred horses pranced and stamped. Tears slipped down her cheeks while she ran her hands over their flanks. She hitched them to her copper chariot and raced to her beloved apple orchards.

Saule cried for the wonderful open sky. She cried for the delicate silver leaves of the oak and the massiveness of its iron roots. She cried for the apples spoiled and shriveled on the ground. She filled the hillsides with the red berries of her tears.

To this day, when Saule's people make pies and tarts of her apples and berries, they remember Saule's tears, the time of the tower, and the gifts of the stars. They remember the magic of the Smith of Heaven's Hammer and that succulent, delirious moment of joy when Saule the Sun spun free again.

Solntse, the Girl at the End of the World

Folklore is an originally oral set of wisdoms and stories. The fairytale is often folklore preserved in written form. This fairytale of a traveler finding refuge in a red house at the end of the world, in which an Old Woman lives with her daughter the Sun, almost certainly tells the story of the Slavic Solntse, the Sun Maiden. Solntse reminds us immediately of the Baltic Saule (see "The Sun, the Stars, the Tower, and the Hammer"). But for the Baltic Saule, we need not rely on the code of the fairytale because we have for her explicitly religious poetry.

The hazy origins of the Slavic peoples, on the other hand, far predate the relatively recent advent of record keeping. By 200 B.C.E., these indigenous peoples had settled a huge area, east of the Vistula River and the Carpathian Mountains and west of the Don River, in central and eastern Europe. The descriptions we have of Slavic deities, temples, and religious life were written down by the peoples who destroyed them. Successive migrations of Germanic and Asiatic tribes, themselves pushed out by other groups hungry for room, drove the Slavs north, south, and east, thus mixing them geographically, economically, and culturally with their neighbors: the Balts, the Iranians, and the Thracians (in areas that are today parts of Bulgaria and Turkey).

Missionary treatises describe a pastoral Slavic life in a patriarchal and warlike culture dominated by male gods. Archaeological monuments, reconstructions of linguistics, and fairytales like this one, however, suggest that the early Slavs were agricultural peoples with a matrifocal culture. Another piece of Slavic lore, for example, tells of a male Bright Moon married to a female Sun, whose children are the stars.

The identity of the Old Woman in this story is not clear. But her image recalls that of Mother Night, Mother Holle, or Hel, the Germanic underworld goddess.

The imagery in the "Song of the Wandering Aengus" (see Gregory in Bibliography), by the nineteenth-century Irish poet William Butler Yeats, recalls both Saule and Solntse. And because Yeats costumes the soul as a young girl, Saule and Solntse are suddenly suggested as pictures of the soul as well as the sun.

I went out to the hazel wood,
Because a fire was in my head,
And cut and peeled a hazel wand,
And hooked a berry to a thread;
And when white moths were on the wing,
And moth-like stars were flickering out,
I dropped the berry in a stream
And caught a little silver trout.

When I had laid it on the floor
I went to blow the fire aflame,
But something rustled on the floor,
And someone called me by my name;
It had become a glimmering girl
With apple blossom in her hair
Who called me by my name and ran
And faded through the brightening air.

Though I am old and wandering
Through hollow lands and hilly lands,
I will find out where she has gone,
And kiss her lips and take her hands;
And walk among long dappled grass,
And pluck till time and times are done
The silver apples of the moon,
The golden apples of the sun.

Solntse, the Girl at the End of the World

ONCE A MAN CAME TO THE END of the world. He'd eaten the last of his food, his feet ached, his shoes were splitting, and his body pounded with weariness. Just when the last of his strength had left him, he saw before him a red house. He knocked on its door while the wind whipped his back.

A sob rose in his throat when he thought he heard slow footsteps. Perhaps finally he might find rest.

Indeed, the door opened. An old woman dressed in black peered at him. "You are a traveler?" she asked.

"I have walked from the beginning of the world, Grandmother," he said. "Will you let me stay for the night?"

The old woman closed her eyes and touched his arm. After a long moment, she drew him over the threshold. She held on to him until he'd seated himself on a wooden bench at a table up next to the hearth coals. She put before him a basin of steaming water, a cake of soap, a scrap of cloth, and a rough towel.

"Wash," she said. "My daughter will come soon. Then we can eat."

She sniffed expectantly. The fire pot's aroma wafted about them.

The man bent and removed his worn-out shoes. He pushed up his sleeves and plunged his hands into the water, soaping, and rubbing his face with the cloth. He moved the basin to the floor and eased his naked feet into the hot water.

A sudden warmth flared in the whole room, as if bellows had stoked the coals. A girl in radiant scarlet appeared, though the man had heard neither door opening nor footsteps. Her young face kissing her mother's shimmered before him.

"Solntse, my daughter," said the old woman. "Tonight we have a guest, a journeyer from the beginning of the world."

The girl smiled, and the man saw himself strong again in a summer-lit river long ago. Then he thought he saw diamondlike wings fold into the girl's back. The old woman put food on the table.

As the man dried his face, the towel smelled like summer on the river.

They ate. There was stew and steaming bread. As his stomach filled, a shyness stole over him. He longed to look again and again at the girl's face. But he could not meet her gaze. He slid his eyes toward her that her beauty might stun him secretly.

Supper was finished. The conversation of the two women spilled through the man like warm honey. The young woman's loveliness and his long-delayed comfort melted together inside him. The old woman made a bed for him of piles of quilts. Like a child, he allowed himself to be pocketed in its warmth. With heavy lids he watched while the mother heaved the girl's outer red dress over her head. Its scarlet seemed the glow of a hundred candles as the woman hung it on a hook. The girl stretched her plump bare arms and loosened the gold ties at her bodice. She curled on a bed in the corner across from him and her mother pulled the covers over her.

Then the old woman drew from a trunk a huge dark cloth. She hung it over the glow of the red dress as if it were a bird in a cage she wanted to sleep. Instantly, the house darkened, and the man felt himself drop into the nest of the night.

The man woke in the long blackness to the sound of the old woman's crooning. "Hmmmm, my little girl who sleeps too long. Your hair clings to your cheek, and the quilts crease your arm. Come my Solntse, come my little sun. The night is too long. Rise, my darling, and be off again."

Then he could see the old woman, soft in the red light from the bared dress on the hook. She had tucked into her belt the dark cloth that had covered the dress. She shook her head tenderly.

"Come my Solntse," she sang, "come." Gently, she folded away the covers over her daughter's form. The girl sprang up, teasing, nuzzling her head against her mother while the old woman pushed back, laughing.

Then Solntse tightened her bodice and, like a tiny girl, held up her arms while her mother slipped the red dress over her head. Reddish-yellow light ribboned to the corner where the man lay, his heart bursting with wonder at the curve of what again seemed like wings feathering from her back. The old woman, lower lip held in her teeth, grasped the limp dark cloth at her waist, as if restraining her hands from further help or play.

Then quickly, lightly, as if she had not done it at all, Solntse darted across the room, kissed him, and slipped away through the door. The man could not be sure, but it seemed that the door had not opened, that she had simply flown through its crack. The windows of the little house brightened, and the old woman let the dark cloth fall to the floor while she reached with the other hand to wave.

The Chanukah Story

*Long after their slavery in Egypt, their escape into the desert, and their
own colonizing of other people's lands, the Jews themselves were harshly
colonized by the increasingly powerful Greek empire. The Syrian governor Antiochus heightened to torture and death the penalties for noncon-
formity to Greek ways. He ruined the Jewish temple, which had been
built according to Yahweh's detailed instructions (Exodus 25–27). The
Jews, under Judah the Maccabee, fought a guerrilla-style war against
Antiochus. The war lasted twenty years, but the Jews, after the first
three years, were able to reclaim and renew their temple and to light in
it again the fire of their Lord.*

*Many Jews had been willing for political and economic purposes
to assimilate with the conquering Greeks. But when their own religious
choices were no longer tolerated, such compromise became unaccept-
able. Extraordinary will, persistence, and even war were necessary. The
revamping of the temple is the most celebrated moment of the war
against Antiochus. Chanukah means dedication and renewal. In the leg-
endized version of the story, the people relit the sacred lamp in the temple with enough oil for only one day. But, miraculously, the oil burned
for the full eight days it took to press more oil.*

*Officially a minor Jewish holiday, Chanukah is a celebration of
light during winter solstice. The Catholic or Jerusalem Bible carries two
versions of the Chanukah story in the books of the Maccabees.*

*Although Yahweh is popularly understood as having no image (he
admonished his people in Exodus 20:4 not to make for themselves "any
graven image"), there is evidence that an earlier Yahweh had indeed
allowed his people to make use of earthly images of himself. He had
led his people in their desert wanderings in the form of a pillar-shaped
cloud. He had flamed as a column of fire by night. He had appeared to*

Moses as the mysteriously unconsumed burning bush. Much later, he was represented by the ever-burning fire inside the tabernacle. "Thou shalt make a candlestick of pure gold: of beaten work shall the candlestick be made: his *shaft, and* his *branches,* his *bowls,* his *knops, and* his *flowers shall be of the same . . . "* (Exodus 25:31, emphasis added). The fire in the candlestick seems clearly a metaphor for the spirit. Similarly, the temple in which the fire burns seems easily a metaphor for the body. Body and spirit, bride and groom: this is a wedding of the tangible and ethereal parts of any one person, a wedding of a people with their guiding mythology. The war in this story, beneath its political reality and sadness, is a metaphor for the fierceness of people's struggles to stay united within themselves and with one another, especially in the face of forces that would tear them apart.

The Chanukah Story

THIS IS THE STORY OF A TEMPLE and its fire. Like a miniature world, the temple stood on a hill and its fire burned bright at its center. All around moved the larger world of the people who loved the temple and its fire. But around them moved an even larger world. The people in that world did not love the temple and its fire. This is a story of a dictator and soldiers, a man called Hammer, and a miracle.

The people who loved the temple and its fire were the Jews. They swept the temple's chambers and adorned its halls with ivy. They pressed oil for the fire's lamps and tended the fire so that it never went out. For the Jews, the temple was like a bride, and the fire like her groom. The altar's sea-purple curtain was the bride's flowing dress. The bread for the altar was shaped like the bride's long braids. In the orange-blue flames in the bowls of the altar's golden lamp, the people saw the robes of the groom.

But the Syrian governor, Antiochus, saw the temple like a woman that he wanted for his wife, not because he loved her but because he wanted power over her. The fire in the temple was like a man Antiochus was fighting, and he used every trick he could to win. Antiochus wanted all the worlds to be his. He wanted the Jews to follow his rules and to stop doing what they pleased. Finally, Antiochus ruined the temple and put out its fire.

An old man called Mattathias and his son, Judah the Hammer, fought Antiochus, his rules, and his armies. They went to war to bring back the temple and its fire. They fought so the bride could hold again her groom in her arms.

It happened like this.

One day, long before Governor Antiochus tried to grab all the power for himself, a warrior called Alexander the Greek marched into the world between the three seas. Some people called him Alexander the Great, since he had already killed kings and stolen the riches of many nations. The Jews were afraid. Maybe Alexander would try to take their temple with its fire.

But the priest of the temple swallowed his fear. He brought Alexander gifts and welcomed him. Alexander took the gifts, but he did not touch the temple or its fire. Alexander was tired, and he had seen many worlds cooperate and still remain separate and different. He told the Jews that they must learn of Greek gods, dress in new clothes, and sing new songs. But they could keep their own ways, too.

Many Jews did learn the customs of the Greeks. Others would not because they loved their own so much. "We are not making the Greeks learn our ways," they said. "Why should we learn theirs? Why can't we all just live the way we want?"

"Because the Greeks have the power," answered other Jews. "It is foolish not to obey them. And besides, what harm can it do? Have we not also been allowed to do as we wish?"

But Alexander died, and finally a ruler climbed to the throne of the land who would not let the Jews keep their own ways. His name was Antiochus, and the Jews soon learned to call him the "Mad Man."

Antiochus called himself the "Revealed God." He wanted the Jews to put out the fire in the temple and put statues of strange gods inside it. He wanted the Jews to look like Greeks and to eat like Greeks. Even though Antiochus himself was not Greek, he had adopted Greek customs for his own and wanted everyone else to do so, too.

At first, Antiochus tried to trick the Jews. "You will get rich if you do what I say," he said. "You can play in my sporting events only if you dress exactly as I say. And your only chance of getting treated fairly comes if and only if you obey me."

Some Jews did obey. They thought it too hard to disobey. "Besides," they said, "this way we can live comfortably, we can play in the games, and we can get fair treatment."

"What's fair about it?" asked other Jews. "You're getting fair treatment at the same time that you're being treated unfairly. What kind of sense does that make?"

Even when many Jews did obey him, Antiochus was never satisfied. He invented terrible punishments for people who did not obey. And he decided to take the temple of the Jews for himself. Antiochus found two priests who would work for him instead of for the temple and its fire. Jason and Menelaus set up statues of strange gods in the temple and gave Antiochus temple riches in exchange for status and power.

But still, some Jews did not obey Antiochus. Finally, Antiochus sent an army to trample the temple's sanctuaries. They snuffed the temple's fire and swept all the holy oil from its shelves. It was as if the bride lay crumpled, her sea-purple dress torn from her body, and the groom lay stunned and ashen, just out of her reach. Pigeons made nests in the ruins and pecked at the braided bread that spoiled on the altar.

Who could have believed Antiochus would go this far? The world of the Jews burst apart. The land shook. Young people fainted. Women's beauty faded. Men groaned.

But the soldiers of Antiochus were not finished. They shoved the Jews against the temple's walls. Then they roasted pork before them, the food that Greeks ate but Jews never touched.

The commander of the army yelled out an order. "One of you Jews must eat this meat! Then, and only then," he said, "will Governor Antiochus leave you alone."

The smoke from the cooking fire wafted out the forbidden smell.

"Eat it!" said the commander. "Just do it, and be done with it."

"We are never done!" shouted an old man named Mattathias. He did not speak to the commander. He spoke to the Jews who clung to one another, their faces frightened and filled with grief. "The bride has been chained and the groom choked! But we are still free, and we must do what is right!"

"What difference does it make?" the commander pleaded. He was hating his job and wishing to go away.

Mattathias spat. "Your rules are not our rules," he said.

Suddenly, a young man dressed in the clothes of a merchant elbowed his way out of the crowd. "Old man," he said. "You're behind the times. The temple is ruined. The fire has gone out. The wedding is off." He turned to the commander of Antiochus's army. "I will eat your meat," he said.

The crowd stiffened. Mattathias's hand disappeared into his robe. The commander, relieved and triumphant, skewered a piece of meat for the young Jew. "You are a sensible man!" he said heartily, and the merchant reached for the fat-dripping morsel.

But before he could taste it, Mattathias, smooth as a fish, stabbed the merchant with a knife. No one at first understood the young merchant's wilting form.

"There's no going back!" roared Mattathias, and he slit the throat of the surprised commander.

Soldiers and people erupted, screaming and moaning. Mattathias, his knife raised, a red stain spreading on his sleeve, shouted for the people to follow him.

Out into the wild valleys and the mountains the people fled, leaving behind their farms and their vineyards.

Governor Antiochus rejoiced. He imagined he had won control of all the worlds.

But Antiochus did not understand Mattathias. Nor did he reckon on the bold trickiness of the son of Mattathias, Judah the Hammer. Judah the Hammer made soldiers out of these homeless people. He turned plows and pruning sticks into weapons and mixed his father's spit with the dirt of the valleys to make courage.

Against Antiochus's armies, with their elephants, chariots, spears, and jeweled armors, three thousand Jews battled with sticks, shouts, and silence. They pounded the Syrians that first spring. Furious, Antiochus added fifteen thousand men to his army. "Smash them!" he ordered.

But Judah the Hammer killed the new Syrian general and took his sword. The sky turned red. The Syrians fled.

Next Antiochus sent twenty thousand men. The Jews hid themselves. The Syrians searched for them deeper and deeper in the valleys. Judah the Hammer swung narrow and hard. The Syrians, used to wide plains for their maneuvers, panicked and ran.

"Then stick to the plains!" screamed Antiochus to his new leader, General Gorgias.

General Gorgias was famous for his clever strategies. He split his army and sent half to surprise the Hammer's troops at sunrise. But the Jews sneaked from their tents, leaving campfires burning as if everyone still slept.

"They've deserted!" exulted General Gorgias. "We've terrorized them."

But General Gorgias was mistaken. Back in his own camp, Gorgias smelled the scent of death. Judah the Hammer had killed the sleeping half of his army.

Even this famous general was no match for this people. Judah the Hammer and the Jews had won.

Now it was time to return to the bride and the groom.

The people fell to their knees before the disgraced temple. They laid their cheeks against its stones and shook with sobs.

Then they gathered scythes, pots, needles, long-bristled brooms and brushes, and rags. They cut away the weeds choking the temple gates. They heaved water again and again for washing, scrubbing, rinsing. They planted new plants. They carried unblemished stones for a new altar. They dyed cloth sea-purple for a new curtain. They polished the shafts, branches, and bowls of the golden lamp.

Finally, the temple was ready for its fire. The temple seemed like a bride again, lips parted, eyes shining, cheeks flushed like a girl's. The people were ready to light again the fire of the groom.

"But where is the oil?" cried the priest. A hush fell as the people realized that the crusted oil they had scrubbed from the floors, poured out so long before by Antiochus's soldiers, had been the last of the holy oil. The priest held up just one small jar. "There is only enough oil for burning this one day," he said.

"But pressing more oil will take eight days," said an old man, his voice trembling.

"We just don't have enough. We cannot light a fire and then let it go out again," said an old woman.

"But the temple is ready. How can we not light the fire now?"

Then it seemed as if the temple spoke. "Never does there seem to be enough. You had not enough soldiers, nor enough weapons. But somehow you did have enough. Today is the wedding. Today there will be enough."

The priest poured out that one day's oil for the bowls of the golden lamp. He struck the flint. Orange-blue flames leapt up. It seemed as if the bride's face glowed in the radiance of her groom. It seemed as if the couple's mouths met, full of longing, regret, desire, and joy.

The fire burned in the temple. Yes, the fire burned in the temple. The fire burned in the temple for the second, the third, the fourth, the fifth, the sixth, and the seventh days. The fire burned in the temple for the infinity of the eight days, for all the days the people had feared there was not enough.

On the day of the wedding there is always enough. The fire burns in the temple.

The Christmas Story

The birth of the historical Jesus fell close to an astronomical event that occurs only once every nine centuries. Saturn and Jupiter appeared to nearly touch in the sky on three different occasions: May 27, October 6, and December 1 in the year 7 B.C.E. In a world without electric lights, this conjunction would have been a spectacular sight for anyone looking upward, and it is undoubtedly the historical impetus for the story of the Magi (see "The Story of La Befana").

Four hundred years after the actual birth of the teacher Jesus, the Roman Catholic pope officially changed the meaning of the long-cele-brated Midwinter Feast of December 25. Formerly celebrated as the birthday of the sun god Mithra in the midst of the long Saturnalia holi-day, the Midwinter Feast became Christ's Mass—or the birthday of Jesus.

Mithra had been represented in many forms, chief among them the lion, with the sun, eternal center of the world, burning as his heart. Mithra was boundless time, a silent point between opposites, a winged, invincible soul bursting from the cosmic egg. Roman artists showed Mithra as Oriens, "the Rising One," and Invictus, "the Invincible One." Mithra had ushered in the Platonic Age of Aries the Ram by sacrificing the Bull of the Age of Taurus. His sacrifice was compassionate and meant to bestow everlasting life on his followers.

As Sun wearing a radiant crown, holding the globe itself, with a vanquished enemy at his feet, Mithra served an age of increasing empha-sis on monotheism. Bent on colonizing the known world, Rome folded into Mithra images of many other deities. So central was Mithra as a re-ligio-political image that his influence on the new monotheistic religions was guaranteed.

Thus, Jesus began the new Platonic Age of Pisces the Fish by sacrificing himself in the lamb form of Aries the Ram. He, too, is depicted as a savior who bestows everlasting life, a celestial power, a representation of supreme harmony, and a metaphor for the actual sun. The Gospel of Thomas, rejected for the official version of the New Testament during the political struggles that solidified the Church's power, places these words in the mouth of the mythological Jesus: "It is I who am the light which is above all. It is I who am the All. From Me did All come forth, and unto Me did All extend. Split a piece of wood and I am there" (The Gospel of Thomas, verse 77, in Robinson).

The Roman Saturnalia holiday had extended from November 30 to February 2. The Christian church repressed Saturnalia's wild parties, which allowed slaves to become masters and everyone to freely make love. But it preserved Saturnalia's custom of wealthy people giving gifts to the poor. It also enthroned Mary as a new form of the great Earth Mother Goddess. Just beneath the surface of the new story of a virgin girl impregnated with the light of the world was the old story of the Great Mother of life who self-impregnates or mates with her own Son/Sun, the Year, to give birth again to the light's cycle of life and death.

The Church also unsuccessfully tried to ban the evergreen decorations that had long been popular at ancient yule feasts. The holly and the ivy had been solstice season decorations long before the assertion of the nativity scene. Before holly was Christianized to represent the crown of thorns with its drops of blood, it was a symbol of foresight for the coming year. Matthew 1:18–25 recounts the story of Joseph, who plans to divorce Mary quietly after discovering that she is pregnant. But an angel comes to him in a dream and urges him to stay. Ivy, with its twining properties, was a symbol of fidelity and marriage. Holly and ivy are both evergreen; both are planted to protect the house against which they grow.

The Christmas Story

O N A DEEP BLUE NIGHT LONG
ago, stars clustered in the
heavens in a way that no one had
ever seen before. Light streamed
from their centers like the strands of a web, so brightly that the sliver
of moon in the sky seemed but the discarded rind of a pale fruit. Far
below, a woman alone in an enclosed garden huddled inside her
cloak. She felt wonder and foreboding as she gazed at the strangely lit
sky. Around her, the roses and the hawthorn flowers, red, pink, and
white in the daytime, bloomed purple and gray in the darkness.

The woman was named Mary. She was soon to wed. Unable to
sleep, she had come to the garden to be comforted by its scents and
quiet. But a dog barked repeatedly, and the sky itself discomforted
her. The rocks on which she sat felt hard and sharp. She looked away
from the sky, and unbound her long hair, fingering its sweet-smelling
waves. She felt the weight of incompletion inside her. Things unsung,
unstitched, unpolished lay in her heart. She feared that the coming
marriage might prevent her from ever turning to them.

Silently, she began to weep, brushing her hair from her face, turning her eyes again toward the weirdly lit sky. Suddenly, its web of silver seemed to rain out gold, and there appeared before her a man with wings of lilies. The sheen of the wings was bright white even in the darkness. A wind rustled through the black spread of an oak, and Mary felt her heart pound.

The man's hands glowed red, as if cupping flames.

Mary trembled.

"Fear not," said the man. And out of the cup of his hands flared a red lily. Speckled and curving, it fanned larger with each of the woman's quivering breaths.

"There will fly through the door of you, Mary, the sun child of the world. Your dark is now filled with the seed of the light."

Mary covered her face with her hands and saw the petals of the red lily close about her. She heard a music hum and felt the petals' delicate hold. Something ragged inside her felt mended; something that had been dull now shone. When she opened her eyes, the angel, for surely this winged man had been an angel, had disappeared.

Later, Mary spoke only of the strangely lit sky. She could not bring herself to speak of the angel, though she felt life quicken inside her. Even after she married the man called Joseph, it was not until he understood that she was already with child that she tried to tell him of the rain of gold and of the winged man who had told her she was to mother the sun.

But Joseph's heart was sore with disappointment and reproach. He just could not believe this story, though she begged him to believe. He could not look at her. He went away to his room, which was hung with tools and smelled of shaven wood.

He sat for a long time, his hair falling over his face as he held his head in his hands. Outside, the starlight shafted so brightly that he did not light the oil lamp. By the stars' luminance alone, he stared at a table with unfinished joints and naked, jutting legs. He must leave her quietly, he decided, so that neither he nor she be shamed. Finally, sad and weary, he slept.

He woke in the night to the smell and glow of fire, but there were no flames. Suddenly, a man stood before him in a coat of white lilies. His lips were parted as if he had already spoken.

"Come," said the man. His hands were bright as fire. "You are reluctant and disappointed, Joseph. But come stand with her anyway."

Joseph felt himself flush with heat and argument. Then all around him the night flooded blue and cool. The man in the lilies faded away.

Joseph sat awake until the cock crowed. Then he found Mary in the garden, among the roses and the hawthorn, under the spread of the oak. Her hair hung loose about her. Leaves floated in a pool at her feet. She stood to greet him, her eyes full of tears.

He took her face in his hands.

She held tightly to his forearms.

"The angel came to me, too," he said.

"I need you," she whispered. She reached up to smooth back his hair.

They clung to each other, then eased themselves to the ground, sitting side by side and rocking together.

Later, almost without speaking of it, they cut and singed away each other's hair with sharp broken rocks and a burning stick from the hearth inside.

A breeze blew up and swirled away their locks of hair, carrying them over the gates of the garden and out into the world. Every place the hairs touched the earth, there sprang up holly and ivy twining round each other, green and strong.

Weeks passed by and the couple's hair grew again. They filled a skin bag with coins and went away to pay their taxes. Mary wrapped herself in blue, Joseph in red. Mary, now great with child, rode a donkey. Through cold and wind they toiled up steep hills and through exposed valleys. The beast's neck hairs separated wet with his sweat. They swayed and plodded, ate and slept, the three of them leaning against one another for warmth.

On the night they came to the town of Bethlehem, the couple saw the stars form themselves again into that wondrous web of light.

Suddenly, Mary knew this to be the night of the birth. But they could find nothing but an animal stable in which to pass the night.

The stars were so bright that they lit the stable through the chinks in the roof. In a manger filled with pointed yellow straw, Mary made a bed for the sun child who was to come. The cattle lowed. Mary lay back in Joseph's arms. The horses whinnied softly. The donkey munched. The warmth of the animals heated the tiny room.

From the breast of a hill near the stable, music piped thinly. By the glimmer of a small fire, a shepherd fluted while his companions slept. The sheep shuffled and bleated on the slope. The stars seemed like streams of milk pouring from the udder of the night.

Suddenly, there appeared before the shepherd, in robes the color of milk, a man with wings the color of fire.

The shepherd cried out.

The milky, fiery man pointed one hand to the sky and the other to the ground. The strange milky web above his head seemed to shine even more brightly.

"A child in a manger is born this night," said the man. "A child who will light up the world. Go and look. Find the new light in the stable."

The milky, fiery man disappeared, but the web of light remained.

The others woke to the singing of the shepherd, whose sounds were filled with the wonder that follows fear.

Driving their sheep before them, the shepherds set out for the town. In a stable, they found a man and a woman with a child in a manger. The sheep pressed in a hot circle around them.

In the morning, the cock crowed, and the sun rolled into the world like a tiny king. The doves purled. The horses knelt. The cows bowed to the east. And everywhere blood red berries burst upon the holly.

The Story of La Befana

Not until the fourth century did the pope adopt December 25 as the birthday of Jesus. Prior to that, December 25 had been Mithra's birthday (see introduction to "The Christmas Story"). Early Christians used instead January 6 to celebrate Jesus' birth. January 6, the birthday in Alexandrian Egypt of Aeon, the personification of Infinite Time, also marked Jesus' baptism and his changing of water into wine at the wedding of Cana. This miracle linked Jesus to Dionysus, the Greek savior-god, king of transformation and the vine.

In today's Italy, January 6 is the Feast of the Three Kings. La Befana is the Santa Claus of Italy, who, at the instigation of the Magi, flies about everywhere looking for the Christ child. In some tellings of the legend of La Befana, the wise men are named: Kaspar, Mechior, and Bathasar. The bones of the Magi—a Persian word from which English derives the word magic*—are said to be buried in the cathedral at Cologne. The image of this beneficent old hag, in legend difficult to date and variously told, is a satisfying addition to the images of Virgin and Mother that usually dominate the Christian view of the divine feminine (see "Baubo's Dance").*

Befana means "epiphany." An epiphany is that weird flash when all the pieces unexpectedly fit together. La Befana has led, day in and day out, her usual life. But one day, the Magi come by her door. For these pilgrims, the stars point delicate fingers toward the Christ. Through the voice and the eyes of a child, Befana can suddenly hear and see something else. The ordinary is haloed. We can fly even when we're standing still.

The Story of La Befana

L A BEFANA IS A TALL OLD
woman with a red shawl
and a bent branch broom
that goes sweep-swep-sweep.
La Befana lives in a thin wooden house in the shadows of mulberry
trees whose branches droop with catkins and dark purple fruit. When
the mulberries drop their leaves, La Befana sweeps them, sweep-swep-
sweep, into piles that crackle and crunch. Another tree by the door of
her house never drops its leaves. Its arms are heavy with sweet fat
oranges.

La Befana has a long nose and a hump on her back. Her hands
are speckled with pale chocolate. She pins the white billow of her hair
with combs made of bone. Befana's kitchen shelves are libraries of
jars and tins. Honey, almonds, hazelnuts, and the skins of lemons and
tangerines. Cloves, vanilla beans, and cinnamon. Sugars and flours
piled up like mountains, with chipped rosy teacups for scoops.

Up until the winter of our story, La Befana had swept and baked
for no one but herself. Sweep-swep-sweep went her broom, year after

day, day after year. Spicy, doughy smells curled out of her windows as she baked. Knead-knod-knead went her hands on the breads, knead-knod-kneading the yeast and the sugar. Sometimes she stepped from out her round-topped door, red shawl over her head, to gather wood for her fire. Clack-drack-clack went the sticks for her stove.

La Befana never spoke. People heard her noises, but they never heard her voice. At least, people could not remember the last time they had.

But one year in wintertime, when the leaves dried in yellow-brown piles and the oranges were swollen and fragrant, Befana had a conversation. Everyone heard her. And then, not so long after, Befana forever changed her bakings.

One fine morning, a strange parade marched down the mulberry street. Everyone watched. They held one another and shouted and crowded at the edges of the procession. La Befana stayed inside, but she parted her curtains and stared.

She saw animals and people. Turbans and chests. Milling and swarming. Children racing. Jewel-colored flags. A black cat the size of ten house cats walked liquid as soup next to enormous clopping brown beasts with knobbed knees and noses and bumps on their backs. Cases carved with suns and crescents thumped the sides of the brown giants with each huge mincing step they took. An old man in red at the front; a younger, head wrapped in a pillow of purple, at the middle; and a third, robes green as the orange tree leaves, at the rear. A boy plucked a stringed box that made the sound of happy crying. Another shook bells tied with red ribbons to a stick.

Befana's breath frosted her window. She rubbed it clear with her fingers. At that moment—everyone saw it—a child sprinted out of the throng straight to Befana's door. He hopped from foot to foot there, bundled in gray wraps, knocking—knock-kneck-knock—at her door.

La Befana cracked the door, then opened it wide enough to show herself, her hand clutched around that bent branch broom. The music stopped. The parade paused. It was as if even the strangers knew that La Befana needed a silence in which to try out her words.

Everyone saw the little boy reach for the hand that held the broom. People saw La Befana's hand tighten on the old bent branch. But she gave him her other hand, closing his little one in her own.

People puffed with breath they did not let out.

The child spoke first.

"We're looking for the Royal Child, Grandma. We're looking for the Royal Child who will light up the world."

People's breaths went out and in.

"Eh?" said La Befana.

"We're looking for the Christ, Grandma. Come with us. We're bringing the Royal Baby our gifts."

Befana was silent. The little boy's head tipped up to her face. "Come, Grandma," he must have whispered again, because then La Befana spoke, her voice husky with years of no use.

"I have my sweeping," she said.

"Please," said the boy.

"I have my baking, child," said La Befana. "I have to gather the wood."

And then the boy held her. He wrapped round her gray skirts and clung to her. Everyone watched her set away the broom and rest both old hands on the child's small back.

Then somewhere in the clear air the music started again. As if they were dancers, the people and the animals in the parade pivoted, began to jostle and to call out to one another. The boy unstuck himself and plunged away. Befana stood for moments with her hand around an orange before she plucked it and shut her door hard.

The sounds of the bent branch broom began again. Sweep-swep-sweep, sweep-swep-sweep. But the sound smudged a little: Sweep, swep, swep. Swep. Swep—as if Befana were leaning and thinking.

If you had peeked in at the window, you could have seen her dreaming there, leaning on the broom. Her eyes like butter melting; her tiny images, mirrored in the library of kitchen jars, very still. Then, suddenly, Befana and all the mirrored Befanas began to move. And all around, the kitchen moved, too.

Lids clattered from tins. The rolling pin danced. Eggs burst themselves in red and green bowls. Beat-bet-beat, knead-knod-knead went Befana's hands. Cloves and cinnamon swirled through the air. Rinds of lemons and oranges scattered like commas and parentheses onto pages of rolled out flour. Vanilla beans shivered in snowy sugar. Almonds and hazelnuts cavorted in honey. Cream frothed. Chocolate slivers spun from the backs of Befana's hands, drifting onto balls, twists, and mezzaluna rolls of cookies and cakes. The hot oven mouth closed on them all.

Befana packed a basket. Layer after layer, lie-lo-lee, of cookies, cakes, and candies she packed. Sweet, steamy scents careened out the windows.

Then Befana washed her face with water from a gray wood bucket. She gazed at herself in a jar of orange peels. She smoothed her hair and pinched her combs tight. She pinned the red wool shawl at her throat. Then she rested her fingers on her eyes.

Finally, La Befana took up the basket and opened her door. She had her gifts for the Royal Child. But it was twilight now, and a red ribbon on the street was all that was left of the parade. Could Befana catch up? A mulberry leaf settled like a crown at her feet.

La Befana disappeared and returned with the broom. She began to run. The basket bounced at her side. She wheezed. She ran and she ran, and then, suddenly, a gust caught her. The broom tilted and lifted. La Befana flew away up high into the stars.

La Befana is a tall old woman with a bent branch broom that goes sweep-swep-sweep. She lives in the shadows of the mulberry trees, and she bakes and gathers wood and talks not much at all. But ever since that winter, Befana packs every year a basket of gifts— cookies, cakes, and candies—for the baby Christ.

La Befana never catches up to the parade. But she flies each year across the sky, stopping at every house below. She is looking for the Child who will light up the world. La Befana is never sure what the Child may look like. So she leaves her gifts at every home, in case the child within is the king or the queen of light.

Raven and the Theft of Light

FROM THE INUIT PEOPLES, NORTH AMERICA

Modern science's chaos theory, first developed in the 1970s, pictures the world not as a predictable machine but as great fields of energy that constantly flow and pull themselves into tangles and furrows—unrestrained, irregular, and eternally creative. Chaos is the name of the force that gives pattern and shape to random flow. Everything, posits chaos theory— from swirls of cigarette smoke to the dripping of a tap, to waves of grief, to the growth of an organization or a relationship, to the color splashes of math equations turned into computer images—has a rhythm, which continually divides and mutates into eddies, vortexes, and rolls. The tiniest shifts in these rhythms multiply to totally unpredictable outcomes. What seem like static, predictable shapes and processes—from earthquake zones to divisions of arteries, veins, and capillaries in the circulatory system, to the formations of snowflakes—formerly stuffed without question into the perfect shapes of Euclidean geometry are far more accurately described by chaos theory's fractal geometry, which attempts to picture mathematically the endless meldings, branchings, and shatterings of the rhythms of chaos. The old scientific paradigm pictured the world as a giant machine that ticked and hummed endlessly while humans simply fed it more fuel and studied its interlocking parts. Chaos theory now pictures the world as alive, powered by a mysterious, primordial force limited only by entropy—or the ultimate waste state of all energy use and the death of all processes.

The ancient religious archetype of the Trickster is uncannily like a personification of modern chaos theory's primordial life force. The Trickster lives at the edges of boundaries. He is the misshapen one who ends up being strongest of all. Ever mindful of slowing the arrival of entropic death, he is always conserving energy—fishing treasures from the trash heap, never failing to snooze and snack, always fooling with new ways to do with less. Trickster or his tricks show up again and again in solstice tales. It is as if the ancients knew all about chaos at the boundaries of life and invented Trickster to describe the way we make the shift from one state to another. We slip and slide to a new place, folded up inside of ironies, our rules scuttled and plans squashed. But we moderns forget to ask for Trickster's help, or if we do remember, we try to get him to work an eight-hour day with extra commute time. So when Trickster arrives, as he always does, we're shocked by his simplicities. He kicks back, tells stories, insists that we pay attention to our bodily needs and desires.

Raven, the Trickster in this North American Inuit story, is as self-interested as a child waiting for Santa Claus. He, too, is inextricably nested in community, overflowing with himself, and tenderly loyal. Only when his people are well, after all, can Raven's pleasures—vittles, bedding, shiny things, and talk—be secure.

Largest member of the crow family, the bird raven is bold, gregarious, intelligent. A spectacular, long-winded flier, with a song that ranges from screams to whispers, the raven can solve puzzles, imitate other animal sounds, and often mates for life. Both father and mother ravens feed their young. Raven is at home in high mountains, boreal forests, rocky sea coasts, and treeless tundra.

In this wonderful story, of which there are many different tellings, Raven's brilliant trick is to turn himself into a baby, saving the day by his simple, ravenous, squalling, demanding, endearing being.

Raven and the Theft of Light

Iᴺ ᴛʜᴇ ᴛɪᴍᴇ ʙᴇꜰᴏʀᴇ ᴛʜᴇ stars, and before Tupilak stole the moon and the sun, everyone lived on this side of the sky. Tupilak was a magician with a high cone hat from which he could turn endless fountains of water, and shoes that could walk miles in a step. One harsh winter, when the snow froze the very earth, Tupilak used his power to cut a hole in the sky. Then he climbed through and built himself a house on the other side.

His wife argued with him. "What are you doing?" she cried. "All our friends are on this side of the sky. You're setting us up to be completely alone."

"You can go back and visit," he assured her.

"I don't want to visit. I want to be here right next to everyone and everything. I don't want to live alone!"

"What do you mean, live alone?" said Tupilak. "You'll be living with me! And we'll have children, and the whole thing will be much more comfortable. Why, everyone else will want to visit you!"

"But no one has your magic, Tupilak. They won't be able to come."

"Oh, probably some of them do," he said, and persisted in his plan. He carried from the first world all his magical tools. His wife, sighing with resignation, carried a stash of frozen seal meat.

After they had settled as best they could, and had even had a beautiful daughter, Tupilak could see that his wife was still sad and dissatisfied. In order to please her, he decided to steal the light. He climbed through the hole in the sky, and into each of two strong bags, wrapping their necks tight with sinew rope, he crammed the moon and the sun. He pushed the bags through the hole and hooked them high on the ceiling of his house, letting out the light only when he chose to do so.

Now, the world on this side of the sky had no light at all. Because Raven loved to sleep, he hardly noticed at first. Whenever he awoke and saw that it was still dark, he snuggled into his cozy snow hut and slept again. He dreamed of steaming globs of fat, succulent fish morsels and of turning breathtaking somersaults.

But the people were puny and tired with lack of light and food. They didn't even have the strength to wonder anymore where Tupilak and his wife had gone.

But when the people came to Raven, interrupting his dreams, calling weakly at his door, Raven thought of Tupilak. He picked his way through his collections of shiny treasures and poked out his head.

"Raven, the sun never comes out anymore—and there's no moon either. We're running out of food."

Raven heard the despair in their voices. "I'll bet Tupilak's behind all this," he muttered. Out loud he promised the people that he would try to find the sun.

"And the moon," they said.

"The moon, too," he assured them.

"A pretty puzzle," thought Raven. "This is probably going to be a long journey." So he took as big a bag of food as he could carry and, in another bag, several good-sized rocks. Then, increasingly roused at the idea of outwitting Tupilak, Raven pulled down his beak, drew on his magnificent black-winged coat, and soared into the freezing night sky.

Whenever he needed to rest, Raven dropped a rock from his pack into the endless dark waters below. The rock changed—kerplash!—to an island on which Raven could perch, gobbling down suppers huddled in his warm feather coat, until he was ready to fly again.

Finally, he came to the rip in the sky made by Tupilak's magic. When Raven stepped through, he found himself dazzled by the sunlight on the other side of the hole, for Tupilak had let the sun out of its bag for the day. The sky was blue. A pool of water glistened, and plants poked green, red, and pink on the brown earth. Raven saw Tupilak in the distance, unmistakable in his cone hat, soaking up the yellow heat.

Raven coughed.

Tupilak squinted. "That you, Raven?" he called.

"None other," said Raven.

"What do you want?" said Tupilak.

"The sun and the moon."

Tupilak laughed. "Not a chance, Raven. They're mine now."

"You're a thief," said Raven calmly.

"Takes one to know one," grinned Tupilak, and he stuffed the sun back into its bag.

"I'm going to get them back, Tupilak!" yelled Raven into the darkness.

Tupilak let out the moon and the sun several times while Raven, munching and dozing, cast about with one idea and then another trying to form a plan. Then in the midst of the sunshine, Raven was startled by the appearance of a strong, round, lovely-cheeked maiden making her way down to the pool with a water jug in her hand. Could this be Tupilak's wife? Could she possibly have grown younger in all this light? Ah! No. It must be their daughter. She did carry herself with the confidence of a magician's child. Raven blinked. Suddenly, he knew his trick.

Quickly, he balled up his black-winged coat, pushed it under a rock, and turned himself into a tiny feather floating on the still pool.

Tupilak's daughter sat dreamily at the pool's edge. Raven Feather trembled with expectation. He waited long, however, because the young woman sang softly to herself, bathed her feet and face in the pool, and then, musing and sighing, combed out her long black hair. Finally, however, she dipped her jug, and Raven swirled himself inside it. His heart leapt with the perfection of the moment when the woman took from its lip a deep quaff before beginning her walk home. Jubilantly, Raven Feather slipped down her throat. His plan was working!

Sometime later, Tupilak's daughter gave birth to a huge baby boy, whose mother, grandmother, and grandfather were overjoyed. All the pent-up tenderness of these three, alone for so long on the other side of the sky, they poured into the new little boy, who, unbeknownst to them, was Raven in disguise.

His mother nursed him and played with him. His grandmother doted on him. Tupilak adored him. Raven inside his baby form was careful to cry and pester for lots of things so that his little family would get used to giving him exactly what he wanted. He bided his time, though, before he asked for the bags of light that hung from the ceiling.

One day his mother noticed a bump on the baby's forehead. "Ooooo! You've fallen, little one," she crooned, and she nuzzled him and pressed ice to the bump. But Raven knew then that his beak was beginning to bulge, and that he didn't have much more time.

Very soon after, he cried for the moon bag on the ceiling.

"Shh, baby, shh, that's grandpa's bag," said his mother, and she dandled tasty morsels before him, which Raven, of course, ate ravenously. Pleased that her child was eating so well, she bounced him on her knee, calling forth raucous laughter from her round little boy. But soon he began again to wail, waving his chubby little hands upward, and pouring out rivers of tears.

This time, grandma fed him, changed him, and played the bouncing game, but always his sobbing began again, his mouth gasping for air between heaves, his little finger pointing at the bag with the moon inside.

"Papa's out," said Tupilak's daughter to her mother. "Let's let him have it. What can it hurt? It's tied tightly enough."

Tupilak's wife rolled her eyes. "It would serve him right anyway if the thing got out."

So Raven, hiccoughing with joy, was given the moon bag to play with. In seconds, the little boy's face looked round and placid as the moon itself. His mother and grandmother rocked back on their heels, enjoying the sweet silence and the happiness of their little seal pup. The minute their attention wandered, however, Raven unknotted the sinew sure as if he'd had beak and claws, clapping and screeching as the moon sailed out, bouncing through the smoke hole like a ball of blubber.

Tupilak came rushing back to the house when he saw the moon rolling through the tear in the sky. "Who touched my bag?" he bellowed, but stopped short when his wife and daughter pointed to the baby, who had ceased his chortling long enough to emit a shriek of joy upon seeing his grandfather. "Dada!" he called, and reached for Tupilak's old spotted hand.

Tupilak's face softened like a long-cooked stew. The baby cooed and patted his grandpa while Tupilak beamed with pride. The two women looked at each other and shook their heads.

Raven wisely waited, however, before he cried for the sun bag to play with. Then when Tupilak had settled snoring into a nap, he began his earnest howling, waving his hands as if trying to pull down the sun bag.

Tupilak woke up. "Oh, give him anything he wants," he groaned. "Just shut him up."

The two women shrugged and pulled down the sun bag. They each, with tooth and muscle, wrapped and knotted the sinew twice more.

Their closure was so effective that Raven this time could not open the bag. Knowing he must act quickly, he rested regretful eyes for a moment on his mama's back, and then sped, bag in fist, out the door. He raced to his rock and donned the black-winged cape he'd hidden underneath so long before. His beak plunged through his forehead, and Raven took bird form once again. Grasping the sun bag first in beak, then in claws, he dove through the hole in the sky and streaked away to the people, whose eyes had grown accustomed once again to the light of the moon but who still lived without the light of the sun.

Raven felt hunger pangs as he flew. On he flapped, but his stomach growled for food. By the time Raven spied the people below fishing in the crooked river by the light of the moon, his wings were trembling with effort.

"Ga, ga," croaked Raven weakly. "Give me some fish."

"Get your own fish, Raven," said the people. "We hardly have enough for ourselves."

"Please!" begged Raven. "I'll let out the daylight!"

"You don't have daylight, Raven," said the people, forgetting that they themselves had asked him to bring the sun.

Raven cawed with exasperation. He dropped the sun bag, and with his remaining strength, rammed at it three times, pecking in it tiny holes out of which sizzled particles of the sun, tumbling into the sky as sparkling spinning stars.

"Guess he does have something in his bag!" said the people. They rushed to ply Raven with fish.

Raven gorged and sucked every bone slick. Then, full of power, he tore open the bag. Out exploded the sun, while people screamed and covered their eyes. In a very short time, they were able to bear again this stupendous light and gratefully gathered for Raven an enormous and delectable feast.

On the other side of the sky, Tupilak and his family mourned. Some say they got so lonely they came back to this side of the sky. Others say if they came at all, it was to steal the light again. But Tupilak has never been able to take the light for as long as he did that first time. Whenever it disappears and returns again, whenever people watch the moon roll into the sky among the bits of sun that are the stars, they think of Raven. And whenever people hear a baby crying, they remember Raven's great trick on Tupilak.

Seagull's Box

Here is another Raven the Trickster story—this one retold by Gail Robinson and Douglas Hill in a collection called Coyote the Trickster: Legends of the North American Indians. *In this story, Gull is so intent on his own agenda that he can't see what's really going on. Like Gull, we, too, can run our own little internal bureaucracies—private mazes of rules and points for "being good." We can get so caught up in "being admirable" in our own eyes that we become gull-ible: blind to the intentions and even the actual behaviors of others. It's a setup for a date with Cousin Raven. When we can't let go, Trickster energy will outwit us and unfreeze our little claws.*

Beginning in the mid-1700s, the Xa'ida—or the People—known to outsiders as the Haida, were devastated first by Europeans and then by Russians. Never fully subdued, however, the Xa'ida maintain their ethnic identity on the Queen Charlotte Islands—the Xa'ida Gwair—off the coast of British Columbia. Speakers of the Athabaskan tongue and hunters of whale and sea otter, the ancient Xa'ida were superb craftspeople. They are famous for their still-preserved seagoing canoes cut from single cedar logs and their exquisite renderings in wood and slate of tribal founders, ancestors, and guardians—like Cousin Raven.

Seagull's Box

WHEN THE EARTH WAS VERY young, it was dark and cold like a winter's night through all the year's seasons. Gull was the Custodian of Daylight, and he kept it locked tight in a cedar box beneath his wing. Being Custodian made Gull feel very important, and he was not going to lose his position by letting Daylight out of the box.

"He is too vain!" screeched Owl at a meeting of the people upon Meeting Hill.

"We can never travel in this darkness to our half-homes in the south," cried Robin. Her breast was bleached of color for the lack of light.

"Even the dark mosses wither, and food is scarce," whimpered Rabbit.

"One person is like another because I cannot map his face," shouted Bear. "Enemies pretend to be friends to share my blanket and bowl."

"I cannot see my tail to clean it of burrs," whined Fox.

So all the people complained of Gull's arrogance and thoughtless self-importance.

Then Squirrel turned to Raven and said, "Gull is your cousin. Perhaps he will listen to you. Perhaps you can tell him of your cold blood, and your blundering in the darkness, and make him change his mind."

So it was settled that Raven should meet Gull on the Meeting Hill the next day—or the next night, since without daylight there was no difference between day and night.

Gull agreed to come to the meeting. But it was clear when he came that he was not going to change his mind or listen to what Raven said. He had come only because it made him feel even more important to have Raven pleading with him.

"I was made Custodian of Daylight in the beginning of things," said Gull. "I am to keep daylight safe. And I *will* keep it safe." And he curved his wing tighter around the cedar box.

Raven had run out of words to make Gull see the people's need for light. He thought angrily to himself, "I wish this Gull would step on a large thorn."

No sooner had he shaped this thought than Gull cried out, "Squee! My foot!"

"A thorn, cousin?" asked Raven innocently. "Let me see—I will take it out for you."

But of course it was so dark that he could not see the thorn to remove it.

"I must have light to take out the thorn," said Raven.

"Light? Never!" said Gull.

"Then the thorn will remain."

Gull complained, and hopped on one foot, and wept, and finally opened his cedar box a crack, so narrow that out glanced a shaft of light no brighter than a single star.

Raven put his hand to Gull's foot, pretending not to see the thorn. Instead, he pushed it in deeper.

"Squee!" cried Gull. "My foot!"

"More light, more light!" shouted Raven.

And the lid of the box rose a further crack, so that light gleamed forth like a winter moon. Then Raven reached again for the thorn, and pushed it even further into the soft flesh of Gull's foot.

"More light!" roared Raven.

"Squee, squee squee!" screamed Gull, and in his pain, he flung off the lid of the cedar box.

Like a molten fish the sun slithered from the box, and light and warmth blazed out over the world.

It was never recaptured, no matter how loudly or how sadly Gull called to it to return to its safe hiding place beneath his wing.

Maui Snares the Sun

FROM POLYNESIA

We love the folk tricksters Roadrunner and Br'er Rabbit. But as a reli-gious instead of a purely folk archetype, Trickster is an orphan in modern Western culture. Like the mother and brothers of the Polynesian trickster Maui, we disown Trickster's unpromising shapes and opt for saviors in-stead. The savior archetype promises dramatic one-time solutions. But the comic minutiae of everyday life—full of blips, jealousies, and acci-dents—often calls for Trickster's messy magic. A theft here, a little sweat there, bravado when we don't feel it—the tough old grandmother-of-Maui energy that finagles transitions instead of mastering them.

Trickster Maui is the central character in a vast cycle of Polynesian legends. Some of his stories are as close as we get to pan-Oceanic myth. The second largest of the Hawaiian Islands bears his name. We accuse old Maui; we laugh with him. We credit him with the invention of major Polynesian tools, techniques, and cultural values. Though the Maui in the New Zealand myth cycle dies after crawling inside the goddess of death, mistakenly believing he can destroy her, Maui, the misshapen one—man, bird, and foster son of the gods—is alive every time we chuckle through our tears, and every time a dreaded compromise turns out better than we could have ever dreamed.

Maui Snares the Sun

O N THE DAY MAUI-NOT-
what-he-seems was born,
his mother, Hina-of-the-fire,
thought surely he would die.
Maui-last-born looked nothing like Maui-first, -second, and -third-
born. His back and neck were twisted and his hands and feet were
very large. Hina-of-the-fire wrapped him in the hair of her daughter,
Hina-of-the-sea, and left him to die at the water's edge. Her daughter
held her as she wept.

But Maui-not-what-he-seems did not die. A jellyfish washed up
on the shore and cradled Maui in her lavender arms. She delivered
Maui to the gods and goddesses of the sea. Thus was Maui fostered
by the powers of the deepest deep and taught the wisdom of Tama-
nui-ki-te-rangi, his ancestor in the sky.

Maui, foster son of the gods, learned to bait the magic jawbone
with his own blood. He fished up whole islands from the bottom of
the sea. He sneaked into the underworld and teased Mafuike, the

fire-keeper, until she threw after him all her smoldering fingernails. And when the whole world caught fire, it was Maui who called on the rain to extinguish all but the embering fingernails. These bits of fire he hid in the trees, and he taught the humans to call them out of hiding by rubbing one kind of wood upon another.

There came a day when Maui decided to leave the sea and the sky and to look for his earth family. But as soon as he stepped on earth's soil, he felt a terrible weight on his twisted back. The sky was pressing down on earth, stooping the humans and ironing the tree leaves flat as tapa cloth.

"This should not be," Maui thought. So he crouched with the sky on his back, and then sprang up three times on his powerful legs. And the sky, tossed higher than the mountains by Maui-not-what-he-seems, Maui-strong-one, stays high to this day. Only the flat leaves of the trees remind us of the time the sky pressed so low.

Maui-last-born wandered far. At last he spied his three brothers hurling their spears against a huge rock in the game of *riti*. Who could bounce his spear the greatest distance? Maui watched. But when he came near, as if to join them, Maui-first-born pointed. "Hey! Wrong-shape!" he yelled.

"There's a looker for you!" razzed Maui-second-born.

"Who are you, Twisted-neck?" shouted Maui-third-born.

Maui answered with his spear. He shattered their rock into a thousand pieces. "I am your brother!" panted Maui-not-what-he-seems, triumphant.

The brothers glanced at one another in surprise. But they looked away quickly, not wanting to show that they were impressed.

"Our brother!" hooted Maui-first-born.

"Wrong-shape thinks he's our brother!" chortled Maui-second-born.

"You're not our brother!" yelled Maui-third-born.

"Am!" shouted Maui.

"Not!" shouted the brothers.

"Am!"

"Not!"

"Mo*ther!*" shouted Maui-first-born.

Hina-of-the-fire appeared. Maui saw that she was very beautiful.

"No, you are not my son," said Hina-of-the-fire. "My sons are these three."

"Did you not have another son?" asked Maui.

Hina looked at her first three sons and then back at the stranger. Here eyes grew wide and she covered her mouth with her fist.

"Did you not leave him to die at the edge of the ocean?"

All the brothers looked at Hina.

"I thought you had died," she whispered.

"I didn't die," said Maui. "The jellyfish took me in her long wet arms and delivered me to the gods and goddesses of the sea. Tama-nui-ki-te-rangi is my father."

Maui-first, -second, and -third-born looked at one another. How could someone who looked like Maui-wrong-shape be their brother? And how could Twisted-back know Tama-nui-ki-te-rangi?

Hina-of-the-fire drew Maui-last-born to her and wept.

The brothers were sullen even when Maui invented the trapdoor that kept the eels in their eel pots. "Old Maui-full-of-tricks thinks he's something," they said. "Says he raised the sky off the ground and gave us fire. Next he'll want to stop the sun."

Maui's jealous brothers were right. Stop the sun is just what Maui wanted to do. He got the idea from watching Hina at the pounding of her tapa bark. At work all day with her four-sided mallet, she could reach only the middle of the board by the time Tama-nui-a-te-ra, the sun, slipped back into the sea. "Mama," said Maui, "you don't have enough time to finish your work."

Maui's brothers rolled their eyes. "There he goes again," whispered Maui-first-born. "Making good with mama."

Hina-of-the-fire's smile dazzled Maui-last-born. "Oh Maui, you are so right!" she exclaimed. "Tama-nui-a-te-ra makes his way so quickly across the world each day that plants and fruits take years to ripen and fishermen can barely paddle to deep water before the darkness comes again."

Maui raised his eyebrows. "I saw the gods put Tama-nui-a-te-ra on his course," he said. "Believe me, they never meant him to move this fast." Maui flexed his biceps. "Tama-nui-a-te-ra is going to change his dance, or I'm not Maui-strong-one."

The brothers had stopped pretending they weren't listening. Maui-first-born exploded. "You'll be Maui-cinder if you try to trap the sun," he jeered.

"Maui-ember!" taunted Maui-second-born.

"Yeah! Maui-ash!" laughed Maui-third-born.

Maui-last-born stuck out his tongue.

Hina-of-the-fire shook her head. "Maui, Maui, Maui, Maui," she said. She looked thoughtfully at Maui-last-born. "You would try to trap the sun?" she asked him.

"I hate to see you work so hard, Mother," said Maui. "I will make Tama-nui-a-te-ra remember that there are humans down here who need him."

"I believe you can do it, Maui-last-born," said Hina. She motioned for her other sons to keep quiet. "But you will need the magic of your grandmother. She is Ka-hu-a-ka-la and she lives in Ha-le-a-ka-la, the house of the sun. You must paddle your canoe to Ha-le-a-ka-la. There, on the mountain, beside the *wiliwili* tree, you will find the grass house of your grandmother. Ka-hu-a-ka-la rises every morning when the rooster crows and cooks bananas for Tama-nui-a-te-ra's breakfast. Three bunches she puts out; you must steal every one. Then, when she calls you, tell her you belong to Hina-of-the-fire and ask for her help."

Maui-full-of-tricks paddled through the waves and swells to Ha-le-a-ka-la. All the world rejoiced at Maui's plan. The birds sang, the pebbles rumbled, the rainbow shone, and the hairless dogs were seen.

On top of the mountain, by the *wiliwili* tree, the rooster crowed three times. Maui saw his Ka-hu-a-ka-la hobble out of her grass house. Feeling around with her hands, the old woman set out the first bunch of bananas. Maui saw that she was blind. Maui snaked out his big hand and grabbed the bananas. Ka-hu-a-ka-la put out two more bunches. Maui stole them all.

Ka-hu-a-ka-la patted the ground where she had set the bananas. "Where are the bananas I cook for Sun's breakfast?" she cried out.

Maui grinned and kept silent.

The old woman sniffed the air. "I smell a man!" she called out. "Come out, wherever you are."

"You smell Maui-thief, your grandson," said Maui. "I belong to Hina-of-the-fire, and I've come to Ha-le-a-ka-la to punish Tama-nui-a-te-ra. He goes too fast across the world."

"I smell Maui-take-a-dare," said Ka-hu-a-ka-la. "Who says you can change the dance of the sun?"

"I can with your help, Grandmother," said Maui.

Ka-hu-a-ka-la sniffed. Maui could see she was pleased with his answer.

"So!" said Ka-hu-a-ka-la. "You would snare the sun, is it?"

Maui nodded. Then, remembering that his grandmother could not see him, he reached out and touched her hand. "Yes, Grandmother."

"You need sixteen strong ropes," said Ka-hu-a-ka-la. "One rope for each of Sun's sixteen legs. You must weave them from the hair of your sister, Hina-of-the-sea. Come back when you are finished and I will tell you more. Now go! I have Sun's breakfast to prepare."

Maui returned the fat red bananas to his grandmother's hands. Then, deep under water, he collected the hair of his sister, Hina-of-the-sea, swirled in the bristles of her brush. Of Hina's hair he made sixteen ropes with nooses at each end. And then Maui-last-born, ropes piled in his canoe, invited his brothers to help.

The Mauis were grudging.

"Oh come on, you guys!" said Maui-last-born. "With our grandmother's help, we can do it!"

The brothers shook their heads, but they came with Maui to Ha-le-a-ka-la in the darkness of the night. In the morning, Ka-hu-a-ka-la touched each of their foreheads. "You must weave a net," she said. "Like this," and she laced her fingers cunningly. "You must hide in the lap of the *wiliwili* tree—dig yourselves a hole there!" She scrambled to a joint in the mighty roots, just as if she had eyes that could see. "And then," said Ka-hu-a-ka-la, "you must wait with this magic club."

"What's the club for, Grandmother?" asked Maui-first-born.

Ka-hu-a-ka-la snorted. "You think you take Tama-nui-a-te-ra without a fight?"

Maui-last-born took the club. The four brothers wove the net and dug the hole. They strung the net across the top of the mountain and looped it about the trunk of the *wiliwili* tree. Then they hid and waited.

In the morning, Tama-nui-a-te-ra came in a great rush through the crack in Ha-le-a-ka-la.

"Now!" Maui yelled. The brothers leapt out and, as each of Sun's legs got caught, they pulled the nooses tight and whooped.

Tama-nui-a-te-ra bellowed. He struggled and heaved. But the brothers' clever rope trap held him fast and the *wiliwili* withstood the pull of his weight.

Sun's face turned red with fury. "What do you want, you puny ones?" he roared.

"You're not doing your job!" answered Maui. "You hurry and hurry and the people don't have light to finish a day's work. Promise to go more slowly and we'll release you."

Tama-nui-a-te-ra strained at the snare. "I'll do no such thing!" he cried, and he turned his most ferocious heat on the four brothers.

Maui-first, -second, and -third-born shrunk away from the terrible furnace of Sun's anger. But Maui-last-born stood up and began to swing his magic club at Sun's trapped legs.

Whack! Whack! Whack! Whack!

Maui broke four of Sun's legs.

Maui's brothers cheered.

"I will roast you alive!" shrieked Tama-nui-a-te-ra. The hairs on Maui's body singed away. His face began to blister.

Whack! Five! Whack! Six! Whack! Seven! Whack! Eight legs now Maui broke.

"Okay!" screamed Sun. "Stop! Okay! I promise to go slowly across the sky. Let me go!"

Maui and his brothers loosed the Hina-hair ropes. The rooster crowed. Tama-nui-a-te-ra turned one last furious look on his tormentors and limped away to have his breakfast.

Maui and his brothers left the ropes of their sun-trap dangling near the crack of Ha-le-a-ka-la. "Every time he sees it," said Maui-first-born, "he'll remember this day and his promise to the Maui-brothers-four."

Maui-first-born needn't have worried. We sometimes see the Hina-hair ropes of the sun-trap streaming out of Ha-le-a-ka-la. They look for all the world like the legs of Sun.

But Sun could not have forgotten his promise, even if he'd wanted to. It's true that half of every year, Tama-nui-a-te-ra moves as quickly as he always did on his eight good legs. But the other half of the year, he scuffles slowly on his eight broken legs. Then the people have Maui-full-of-tricks to thank for the sunshine that ripens the plants in their season and makes time for the pounding and drying of the tapa and the spearing of the fish.

Fifth Sun

FROM THE TOLTEC PEOPLE, ANCIENT MEXICO

If Tricksters knew they were being analyzed, categorized, and labeled, they would probably scramble like knew analyzed would the mess if whole word labeled they. They couldn't care less if the Meso (or Middle) American Quetzalcoatl is like the Polynesian Maui or not—just listen to a choir of them pondering the question by sucking and blowing on the straws in their mango sodas.

But Quetzalcoatl is like Maui, only without the jokes. He, too, is a god-hero, who takes the shape of a bird, and in this story, of a very ill man. Quetzalcoatl is the bird-snake-water god, credited, like Maui, with basic cultural inventions. But while Maui saves the day with magic and shrewdly applied harshness, Quetzalcoatl saves the day with self-sacrifice. Christian missionaries would never have found Maui similar to Jesus. But they found Quetzalcoatl's stories so like the stories of Jesus that they even theorized that St. Thomas's mission to India must have reached Tenochtitlan.

Both Polynesian and Mesoamerican mythologies picture the whole world as alive. But the Mesoamerican obsession with the meaning of mortal life was unique. They were deeply concerned with the loops of communication between the world of human life and the worlds above and below. They translated their understandings of the intercourse between the realms of body and spirit into psychedelic visuals of flayed gods, flying snakes, were-jaguars, and obsidian butterflies. But because these are pictorial rather than ideographic or phonetic images, their ultimate meanings are like three-dimensional crosswords with endlessly shifting clues.

We do know that in the rural communities that preceded the giant Mesoamerican metropolises, the village shaman was responsible for leav-

ing the land of everyday experience by subjecting his body to severe physical tests. By depriving himself of sleep and food, or by lacerating his flesh, he could then journey in his nagual—or "dream body"—behind the veils dividing the worlds. Through the skill and surrender of the shaman, the people could swim to the roots of the tree of life and soar to eat the fruit of its highest branches.

Quetzalcoatl, the extraordinarily popular, endlessly guised, hero-god of the later, priest-centered, metropolitan cultures, was probably in part a vivid shorthand for the work of the earlier shaman. Quetzalcoatl represented the sinuous sky energies of rains, clouds, and winds as well as the undulating earth body of the world below. Like the shaman who journeyed out of and back to human life, Quetzalcoatl was the go-between, the melder-welder of the mortal and immortal worlds.

The Toltecs first told the story of Fifth Sun. We know little about them, except that they were magnificent architects and sculptors, who used cement, and that they flourished from 900 B.C.E. to 1179 C.E. We know much more, by comparison, about the Aztec, or Mexica, culture, who overlapped and succeeded the Toltecs and preserved this story in their Nahuatl language. Aztec urban roots reach back to 1400 B.C.E., and the rural aspects of its culture go back another thousand years before that.

The Aztec culture, infamous for its extensive and repulsive practice of human sacrifice, was yet strangely earnest and soulful in its pursuit of these rituals. It seems that the Aztec people had lost their sense of the benevolence of the spirit world in direct proportion to their material, metropolitan gains. Instead of the village shaman with his individualistic rites, now hosts of city priests carried out highly stylized rituals that included extreme personal mortifications and the daily sacrifice of countless citizens and prisoners of war. The priests' lacerations of their own tongues and genitals, their bathing in frigid waters, and their superhuman self-starvations echoed the shaman's psychic dismemberments. But now the world tree of life had its roots in an underworld grown distant, hostile, and increasingly thirsty not for communication but for plain human blood. The gods had turned demonic. Simple mortifications were not enough. Nothing less than the heart torn from the body could begin to satisfy them.

The Aztecs genuinely believed that such sacrifice released the human soul into the world of the spirits—but they no longer had the assurance of antiquity that those spirits were essentially kind. The Aztec state declared that the purpose of its existence was to ensure that this feeding of the gods continue. The singular sincerity of this grisly commitment is demonstrated by the fact that the scale on which human sacrifice was practiced was actually far more politically and economically damaging than it was helpful to the Aztecs.

Whatever else their commitment may have meant, the Aztecs insisted on encountering their mortality—the crux of what is tragic and unanswerable in human existence. Today, unless confronted with war, illness, or catastrophe, only the "artist," the "neurotic," the "oversensitive," or the "priest" ponders the strange juxtaposition of life and death.

The story of Fifth Sun is a kind of meditation on the connection of death to life. Four Worlds come and go before Nanautzin, the "Diseased" or "Scabby One," a form of Quetzalcoatl, sacrifices himself to light the Fifth World. For the Aztec, all humans were "diseased" with the stamp of their mortality. This story is a set of Aztec instructions about the necessity of sacrifice for the making whole of spirit and matter, dark and light.

It could be that even for us, Quetzalcoatl is a symbol of the real self who nurtures the Scabby One deep inside. Scabby One is the openly acknowledged wound, the part that no longer has the energy or inclination for falseness and ineffectual structure. Personal and social deaths are necessary for the survival of life. Individual and cultural transformation is a crucible that requires us to live with agony and to die to the old so that the new may live.

In retelling this lost Toltec legend, I have borrowed imagery and rhythmical sounds from the Cantares Mexicanos (Bierhorst), whose ninety-one song chapters are the chief source of Aztec poetry and a monument of Native American literature. The Cantares, rediscovered in the mid-nineteenth century, were written down in the "time between times" after the catastrophe of the Spanish conquest had unhinged the natural and social hierarchies of the Aztec world. The Cantares were probably the cryptic incantations of a secret elite who, by dancing and singing themselves into ecstatic transport, wished to call back the ghosts of the pre-Christian era. Like the Ghost Dance of the northern Plains Indians at the turn of this century (see introduction to "Spider Grandmother Finds Light for Her People"), the living singers of the Cantares aimed to stand for an instant side by side with the dead. Ghost song singers summoned ghost ancestors in the forms of blossoms and birds to overwhelm their enemies. War in the Cantares was a dance enacted to reunite the broken levels of the universe.

But the Cantares did more than enable a passionately nostalgic, symbolic revisitation of the old ways. The singers of the Cantares spoke of the meaninglessness of human existence only in the context of the larger world of divine significances. They were asking the questions that the Aztecs had always asked. What is the reality of the human soul given that we die?

Fifth Sun

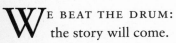

WE BEAT THE DRUM:
    the story will come.
  Toco toco tocoto.
  Toco toco tocoti.
  Tico tico ticoti.
  Tico tico ticoto.
  We beat the drum: the story has come.

Above the frames of flowers, under the sprays of willow and cypress, teeming with parrots and jaguars, scented with jasmine, the gods watched the termination of the first Four Worlds. Out of the shimmering Life Giver, out of Our Mother–Our Father, undulating black and white, out of the Center, slid the first Four Worlds. For each of the worlds, the gods built a sun. But each exploded. The gods watched the worlds come and end.

    The gods built First Sun of Precious Stones. They built the people of ash and fed them only wild corn seeds. But then came drowning waters out of the Life Giver! Everywhere, everything drowning! The ash people of the First World washed away, little black specks, everyone except for those who stayed alive by changing to sleek-scaled fish.

The gods made Second Sun of Burning Flames. They made the people giants who could eat only acorns. How weak the giants of the Second World were! So weak! Ocelots murdered them. Sadly, the gods watched the ocelots suck the bones of the people.

The gods made Third Sun of Darkness. The people were tiny this time, like little seeds in the waters. They ate only pitch and resin. Then the rains poured like fire from the sky, and the Earth opened its black-toothed mouth and swallowed Third World up! Only the dogs, butterflies, and the turkeys were left. Brown, drunken turkeys.

The gods made Fourth Sun of Wind. But the Wind Sun galed and tore the people off the ground. Wind Sun made a hurricane and blew away the faces of the people in Fourth World. It hung the people's bodies, with faces of monkeys now, in the piñon nut trees. Now there were only piñon nuts and monkeys. Only monkeys and the piñon nut trees.

Now, for the fourth time, the skies without a sun staggered like wounded warriors into one another and collapsed. All was darkness.

"Oh, Giver of Life!" moaned the gods. "You are hiding the world in a chest! You are closing the world in a coffer! Giver of Life, you are shrouding the worlds in a grave!"

In the dark, the gods wailed and mourned. They lost themselves in that sorry place where all who have ever lived in a world lose themselves. The goddess with the skirt of fanged serpents, Coatlique, sorrowfully hung a necklace of skulls about her neck. The shell of the back of Tecciztecatl, the man-snail god, turned white as a pile of bones. Quetzalcoatl, the bird-snake-water god, turned his beautiful face to the Giver of Life, trying to see into the shimmering black and the white. In anguish, he covered his face with his hands and fell to his knees. Retching, he tore his own liver from his belly. Like a trembling mouth, the bloody liver bloomed and out of it stepped a young man god, shivering and sick with sores. Thus, Nanautzin, the Scabby

One, was born, chalky white and so ill that the gods could barely look at him.

Nonetheless, they enclosed Nanautzin in their ranks and continued to weep. "There are no people to echo our song!" they cried. "Without the people, our song dies in our throats!"

The serpents on the skirts of Coatlique raised their heads. The goddess opened her mouth. "Fifth World! Fifth World!" Coatlique began a chant to Our Mother–Our Father.

"Fifth World! Fifth World! Fifth World!" the gods took up the rhythm. The serpents on the skirts of Coatlique flicked their tongues and swayed.

The center of the grave of the worlds rumbled. The gods tensed, raising their chant. "Fifth World! Fifth World! Fifth World!"

With a surging, spanging roar, Fifth World, round and enormous, crested from the center of the coffer. The gods sprang and cheered.

New and tender, Fifth World turned beneath their feet. In gratitude they surveyed it and began to plan new people. "This time they must look like us!" they exulted.

Then, excitedly, they bickered and pontificated about the composition of Fifth Sun. "We need something new and different this time. Precious stones did not work! Even Second Sun's fire did not last! Certainly not another ball of darkness! And no more wind suns to blow everything away again!"

Coatlique shouted out, "Nothing but our own blood sacrifice will make a sun to last and last! We must make of ourselves the Fifth Sun for the Fifth World!"

A shrill chant of "yes! yes!—yes! yes! yes!" rose up on every side. The drums beat. Cotoco! Cotoco! "Honor to the Sacrifice! Honor to the Sacrifice!"

Who would it be? Who could it be? On top of a hill, the gods lit a gigantic fire and lined up before it on either side facing one another.

Tecciztecatl, the man-snail god, drew a robe of yellow butterfly wings over his giant shell. He strutted before the company. "I will be Fifth Sun," he boomed. "I will light up the world!"

"Tecciztecatl!" shouted Coatlique. "Make ready to die!"

Tecciztecatl flinched. But he fastened on his neck an ornament of gold. Into his ears he hung jade and turquoise. About his forehead he fixed a crown of hummingbird feathers.

Tecciztecatl made a grand speech. He gesticulated and wrapped his voice around his fancy words. He talked of honor. He talked of his own selflessness. His glittering winged robe ribboned about him. His jewels glistened.

But the serpents on the skirts of Coatlique fell asleep. Nanautzin, the Scabby One, lay shaking despite the heat of the fire.

"Tecciztecatl, enough! Jump into the fire!" shouted the gods.

But Tecciztecatl's knees weakened. He shied away from the flames and started again to talk of how little use he had for fame.

"Enough! Jump!" yelled the gods.

Four times the man-snail god tried but grew afraid and could not jump.

The gods shifted nervously. It was easy to plan a sacrifice, but no one wanted to do it. Tecciztecatl could posture, but he could not dare. Then their eyes fell on Nanautzin, thin and silent at the edge of the gathering. "You! Scabby One!" they called out. "You be the light of the world!"

Nanautzin rose with great effort. "I will do it," he said unsteadily.

Nanautzin did not decorate himself. He did not make a speech. He closed his eyes and turned his face upward. With a last streak of energy, he threw himself into the heart of the fire.

Nanautzin crackled and burned like dry reeds. He burst into a red ball of fire and blasted into the sky.

The gods roared their approval, and Tecciztecatl, ashamed of his cowardice, cast himself, too, into the blaze. But the fire was low now, and the ball he became was not red but the color of ash.

In a riot of exuberance, and embarrassed by their own timidity, the gods pelted the ashen ball with garbage. One flung the carcass of a rabbit who died too close to the flames. To this day, we can see marks of its long ears and feet on the ash-colored moon in the sky.

And so in the Fifth World made of Movement, Nanautzin, the Scabby One, became the Sun and the Light of the World. The man-snail god became the Moon. For everyone still, the Fifth Sun lights the day and the Moon the night. And all the gods rejoice because the people live to echo their songs. Tocoti. Tocoto. Toco, toco, tocoto.

Ra and Hathor

FROM ANCIENT EGYPT

It's no wonder that scholars spend lifetimes studying ancient Egypt, with its nine main deities that fan into dozens of forms. Modern children are another group of people to whom this plethora of overlapping powers and stories makes wonderful sense. After all, children have no trouble crayoning a Sunday School picture of Jesus, for example, in the colors of the rainbow. Like ancient Egyptians, they also distinguish the obvious difference between Sky—that high, blue blanket with its smiling Sun— and nondescript Air. Like ancient Egyptians, they, too, understand that what enters through the head is born much later from a deeper place.

As children, my sister and I, inspired by our stuffed animals, story-books, and the mysteries of the world, invented characters and scenes that would probably have set any ancient Egyptian to nodding sagely. We had a silver trailer that flew in the sky, reachable only by ladder. In it lived a tidy, reassuring woman who ironed clothes; it was guarded by a boy-witch named Ronnie who had only one testicle (I added this detail in an attempt to make sense of some low-toned adult conversation I had overheard). On the earth below, a mother named Lyn Candy forced her children to eat sweets before vegetables, collected rather than eliminated rolls of dust, and supervised her stroke-victim husband, Caleeps. Her daughter Ho-a's mouth had frozen wide open when she disobeyed orders and stuck her head in the freezer. Spotty, her rabbit son, was, of course, the Trickster, who connived ruses and disguises by which he could visit his beloved Karen, a teenager who lay with a broken leg in traction in the hospital.

Our imaginary world at full tilt, my sister and I were introduced, at ages four and five, to an especially fervent worship of the single, three-in-one Christian god.

Similarly surrounded by multiple gods and goddesses, a young pharaoh of the eighteenth dynasty introduced his people to his invention of a single, universal god called Aton. Aton's externalized symbol was a many-armed benevolent sun. The young pharaoh Amenhotep ascended the throne in 1375 B.C.E. during a period of flourishing arts in which Egypt dominated the international scene. Like all pharaohs, he was understood to be the son of the sun god Ra, conceived in union with a mortal queen. The world turned under the rule of Maat, the goddess of Truth, whose eternal, cosmic order guaranteed the security of the human station within that order. Amenhotep came to reign at age ten under the direction of his mother, Queen Hatshepsut, a brilliant, diplomatic woman who counseled concentration on domestic progress rather than on militaristic exploits.

Amenhotep stands out in the four thousand years of Egyptian civilization as the only prominent individual ever to oppose the established regime. Amenhotep, possibly epileptic or oddly shapen of body, rebelled as a teenager against the priests of Thebes by theorizing an abstract ideal that would encompass all the deities in all their forms and rule as kindly as the sun rules in a land graced by a mighty river. He married his sister, the famous Nefertiti, and changed his own name to Ikhnaton, which means "Aton is satisfied." Single-mindedly, Ikhnaton caused the plural word "gods" to be chiseled out of stone monuments wherever it appeared. He founded a whole city of Tell-el-Amarna in honor of this universal god Aton, creator of all things, father and mother of us all. New monuments showed Ikhnaton and Nefertiti standing with offerings while the thousand-handed sun-rays of Aton reach down to them.

Aton was probably the first monotheistic expression in history. One-god would never appear again in a form quite so universal and with so simple a theology. King Ikhnaton, Aton's intriguing first worshiper, was not successful, however, in converting Egyptians to his theology. Egypt's powerful priesthood returned the people to the complexities of their multiple deities as soon as the young pharaoh had died. Quite possibly, worship of Aton was only a religion of the elite even during

Ikhnaton's lifetime. The worship of multiple deities was so well established, and its priesthood so vested in centuries of familial, political, and
military power, that a new religion supported by mere argument would
have taken hold only with difficulty.

Though today Egypt is almost entirely Muslim, the charm remains
of ancient Egypt's multiple conceptualizations of the divine. Indeed,
the idea of a male god who is blind without his female eye rings some
dreamlike truth beside the familiar chant of a one-god as father only, not
mother. Ancient Egypt's pantheon further reverses our culture's expecta-
tions by picturing Geb, the earth, as male, and Nut, the sky, as female.
Clearly, "male" and "female" refer not to actual genders but to polariza-
tions that together form whole concepts.

Because today's records of Egyptian myths often lack coherency, or
because the same story has several contradictory versions, I have taken
in this story small liberties with the flow and relationship of its mythic
elements.

The "male" archetype in this story is understood through a host
of images. As Ra, he is a needy baby, the sun, and a pharaoh. He is a
drudging beetle who methodically and persistently works each day.
Through his mundane, repetitive tasks, he realizes the core of himself,
preserving life by laying his-her egg in his "dung." Out of the nothing,
out of the waste, comes the something, the new. He is a falcon who
proudly soars above his kingdoms. He is a doddering old man, swinging
from petulance to remorse. As Anhur, the "male" archetype is the four-
plumed hero who plays Trickster at the story's end. Anhur is created by
Shu, the male Breath, and Tefnut, the female Tears. Together, Breath
and Tears also form the "female" archetype of Hathor the Cow.

A real-life cow weighs sixteen hundred pounds. She digests eighty
pounds of food each day in a superbly efficient system of four stomachs,
which includes the capacity to filter rocks and metal. The cow turns
plants inedible to humans into essential provisions—milk, meat, and
clothing—making her, indeed, the foster mother of the human race. A
domesticated member of the bovine family (which includes buffalo and

water buffalo), she obliges, like the earth itself, true symbiosis with humans. If we do not take care of her, she will not, cannot, take care of us. Equipped with an astonishingly exact inner clock, she bellows with impatience if not fed and milked promptly twice a day.

The cow archetype in this story shifts form to cat and lion. Playful and soft, the feline is also fierce, jealous, and predatory. She is imperious body, lover of ecstasy and comfort. In this story, she is the eye of the sun, the informant of truth. Whatever may be substituted for that eye is ultimately not acceptable. When the "female" eye of the "male" sun is exiled, only the kindly hero as crafty trickster can enter the dark and unite both poles again.

Ra and Hathor

AT THE VERY BEGINNING, THE blue-green Nun, decked in the weedy rags of the sea, twitched and spasmed, making ready to birth Atum. Atum was the spirit of not-to-be. Atum was the spirit of to-be-complete. At the start of the worlds, Atum curled in the breast of Nun the Deep. Nun moaned and they reeled together, the Nothing Nun and the Something Atum, and because it was time, Atum rose out of the blue-green Deep.

The spirit of not-to-be shrank and dove. The spirit of to-be-complete stretched and floated. A tiny knot grew inside Atum, then loosened and opened like a lotus, petal by petal. Out of the lotus knot slipped Ra, the baby Pharaoh, his single eye shut, and his mouth puckered for sucking. But when no breast delivered milk to Pharaoh Ra, he opened wide his pink baby mouth in his fat baby cheeks.

WAAAAAA!

Out of that round pink cavern streaked the bright round yell of the Sun.

WAAAAAAAAAAA!

Bigger and bigger grew the Sun, until it was Ra, the Man, with a thousand glittering arms reaching everywhere. Reaching and reaching for something or someone. Ra was lonely and he reached up, up, up into the emptiness, until his thousand hands began to numb with the effort.

Then out of the numbness in Ra's hands spurted Shu! Shu was transparent, but his muscles rippled, and he wore an ostrich plume in his flowing hair. They greeted each other, Ra and Shu, yellow Sun and the blue-pink Air. Never to be lonely again, they touched and talked, and cried tears of joy. The tears poured down, down, down. Out of their waters came Tefnut, sister of Shu, dressed in diamonds of rain and dew.

Many-faced Ra, Shu the Air, and Tefnut the Rain started a world. Very early every morning, Ra, like a celestial beetle, rose up in the east, and rolled before him the ball of rich black dung into which he had laid the egg of his fat baby self. All the way to breakfast he pushed his humongous dung ball, light from his beetle belly wrapping it shinier and shinier until finally only its streaming whiteness showed in the sky.

Then Shu and Tefnut, pink-blue and dewy, took off Ra's shiny black suit, bathed the fat baby boy inside and fed him breakfast. They dressed Ra in the wings of a falcon for his flight across the sky. Ra the Falcon surveyed the world, then beat his strong wings and flew straight away. But by the end of twelve hours, Ra was tired. He turned into an old man, his falcon suit draped over the arm that did not hold the cane. Now he was ready to fold himself again into his death egg for his nightly sail into the west.

Sometime in the midst of the next seventeen thousand years, Tefnut and Shu noticed that Ra was no longer a baby every morning. He emerged from his beetle self already old. By the end of twelve hours, Ra was so weak that he could not control the spittle drooling from his mouth. His arms shook and his single eye was dim.

Tefnut and Shu missed having a baby to play with. So they married each other and gave birth to Nut and Geb. Thus, old man Ra became a grandfather.

Though he was peevish, Ra at first enjoyed his new granddaughter and grandson. They were beautiful children who grew rapidly and played joyfully together. Nut was tall, dark, and starry-eyed. Her brother, Geb, hairy and slow, was dressed in green leaves.

But Ra grew weaker and more and more unreasonable. When Nut and Geb one day asked to marry each other, Ra brandished his cane.

"You will not marry!" he shouted.

"Why, Grandfather?" they pleaded.

"Because I said so!" he roared. Then he ordered Tefnut and Shu to tear their children apart.

Tefnut and Shu tried to argue on behalf of the lovers. But, dim though it was, Ra's terrible eye bored into them both. They saw that they would have to obey, but before they did so, Shu took the ostrich feather from his hair. He blew on it and Tefnut wet it with her tears. The one feather became four. A Man and a Cow grew beneath the plumes. They named the man Anhur. Anhur was dressed in a robe with bright designs embossed on its edges. He held in one hand an upright tambourine called a sistrum. In the other, he held the golden rope that was tied to the neck of the celestial Cow. The cow's name was Hathor.

Tefnut and Shu put their arms around Hathor and Anhur. "Some day Ra and all the world will need your help," they whispered. "Wait, and do not forget." Tefnut and Shu drew back. Anhur nodded his head gravely. Hathor assented by blinking her long-lashed eyes.

Then Tefnut, tears glistening, and Shu, muscles rippling like a great wind, obeyed Ra's order. They tore Geb away from Nut. Nut became our Mother the Sky and Geb became our Father the Earth.

But as the words of a hymn are without the music of the sistrum, so were the lives of Nut and Geb without each other. Such was the agony of their longing that even Ra could not bear to see it. With a cry of remorse, he plucked out his single eye.

In the last blink of Ra's sight, Anhur and Hathor looked at each other. Anhur shaped his mouth into the word, "Now." Hathor stepped forward in the dark. Anhur began to hum and to rattle the metal discs on the bars of the sistrum. Hathor, the celestial Cow, began to dance. The old Pharaoh Ra turned his head toward the music, and Hathor distended to him her udder. Anhur sang a song of a cow's rich milk and of a pharaoh reaching for his life. Trembling, Ra felt for the teat and began, like a baby, to suck.

Behold! The old Ra's white hair turned gray, then brown, and then to the fuzz of a child! And so it was that Ra became young again, and Hathor the Cow came to live as Ra's new Eye.

Hathor the Cow was the Eye of the Sun. Out of her udder, she poured milky tears for all that had passed, tears that grew into everything that lives.

Twice each day, Anhur carried to Hathor nine hundred pounds of fodder. He swept her bed a thousand strokes and washed it fresh and clean. Hathor lay like a queen, lifting her chin for Anhur's hard scratching. In all four of her stomachs, Hathor ruminated about the ways of the world.

After much thought, Hathor the Cow one day stamped her hoof nine times. Her cow robes slipped away and she became Hathor the Cat. Anhur was startled. But Hathor the Cat winked at him, and Anhur shrugged. Cats, after all, were much easier than cows. Anhur grabbed a pillow, snuggled under his heavy, embroidered robe, and fell snoring into a deep sleep. Hathor glanced one last time his way, then licked her paw. She purred out an order.

"Nut, my sister," said Hathor the Cat, "you shall be miserable no more. Though you are separated from your Geb, I give you the ability to arch your spine like I arch mine. That way you shall never be completely apart."

Nut felt her heart swell. She smiled. Then she arched her back.

"Shu and Tefnut," Hathor added, turning to the transparent, strong man and the silver-garbed woman, "both of you hold her up."

And so it was that Nut, our Mother Sky, curved herself over her husband, Geb. Supported on the upstretched arms of her father, Shu, and her mother, Tefnut, she stretched to Geb her fingers and toes. Geb, our Father Earth, rose up on his mountainous elbows in longing expectation of his beloved wife's touch.

Hathor the Cat made another decree. "Ra," she purred, "from now on you shall slip each morning from between the legs of Mother Sky."

And so it was that Ra sailed west each night into the mouth of Nut and was caught each morning by Tefnut dressed in her sparkling gown of dew. Then as Beetle-boy Ra, and Falcon Ra, he moved over the twelve kingdoms below, stretching forth like a thousand hands his glittering warmth. All the living beings on Father Earth intoxicated themselves in the temple of Ra the Sun and Hathor, his Eye, drinking and feasting, dancing to the music of the sistrum, dreaming and gaming in the light.

But after five hundred years, Tefnut grew tired of holding up our Mother Sky. She rained out her sorrow. "Can we never rest?" she cried out to her husband, Shu. "Must we hold up Mother Sky forever, and never again have the chance to cling to each the way we once did?"

Shu grunted. His arms, too, ached from his effort. Nut heard them speak, and her heart leapt within her. Surely, if her arch were weakened she could press more closely to her husband, Geb! So she encouraged her parents to slip away.

Tefnut and Shu eased their daughter down and swam away together into the blue-green deep of the Nun.

Hathor, Eye of the Sun, saw Nut wrap herself close to her beloved Geb. She squinted, trying to see where Shu and Tefnut had gone.

But Hathor said nothing to Ra, so he did not notice the change until it was time for his night's passage into the west. He expected his usual smooth journey through Mother Sky. He expected to sail like a boat over phantomless and serpentless waters. But instead, his boat seemed to buck and lurch, and strange cries burst around him. Ra could hardly breathe. Inside the darkness, he panted out to Hathor, "What has happened?"

"Shu and Tefnut went away," Hathor told him. "Geb and Nut have claimed each other again."

"You must find them!" choked Ra. "Or I cannot be born."

"You can be born, Ra," said his Eye, calmly. "It will just take longer."

"It hurts!" moaned Ra. "Find them, my Eye. Bring them back."

Hathor considered. "How shall you see while I'm gone?" she asked.

Ra heard jealousy in Hathor's voice. "Hathor, my queen, my Eye, I shall be lost without you," said Ra as soothingly as he could. "So you must hurry back."

Hathor narrowed her Cat's eyes. "I am not used to taking orders, Ra," she said imperiously. "I shall take as long as I need."

Ra was born, but very late every morning. "If only I could see," Ra muttered. Forgetting that the squeezing and constriction came not from his blindness, but from Mother Sky's cuddling with Father Earth, Ra called for a substitute eye.

No one remembers whom he called to restore his sight. But they do remember that when Hathor finally returned, carrying Shu and Tefnut like kittens in her teeth, she found Ra not forlornly waiting but happily painting streaks of colors across the robes of Mother Sky.

The heavenly Cat dropped Shu the Air and Tefnut the Rain. Her small paws grew huge as a lion's and she lunged after Ra. Gripping Ra in her powerful jaws, she bounded forth from heaven to the land of Nubia where all was dark. Thus the light went out for all beings living on Father Earth.

Shu and Tefnut were once again holding Nut above Geb. But no longer did Ra come forth each day, and the twelve kingdoms grew barren and cold. Nun and Atum, the Nothing and the Something, helplessly cradled the world.

But one day, they thought to whisper: "Anhur!"

No answer. "Anhur!" they called, more loudly this time.

Shu the Air, Tefnut the Rain, Nut the Sky, and Geb the Earth heard them call. They joined their voices and yelled for Anhur. "Anhur! Anhuuuuuur!"

Finally, Anhur, who had been sleeping all this time, woke up. He stretched and tried to see in the dark.

"Anhur!" shouted the gods and goddesses. "You can't see anything because Hathor has taken Ra away to Nubia. You've got to help, Anhur. Bring them back!"

Anhur roused himself by washing his face and combing back his black hair. He smoothed his warm robe about himself for the long cold journey and felt the four plumes on his head to make sure they were straight. First he took up a huge skin of beer. On second thought, he dyed the brew dark red and then packed three cakes each of barley, millet, and wheat, the sistrum, and the golden rope. Then he turned down the rocky path that led to Nubia.

Finally, he arrived in the land of the caves. He wandered among the shadows until he saw a glow around a corner. There sulked Ra, thin and listless, with a huge lion pacing beside him.

Anhur watched, hiding himself in the shadows.

"Pleeeaaase, Hathor! Let's go back," Ra whined.

The lion did not answer. She turned away from the thin pharaoh and lay down, tail switching with irritation.

Anhur raised his eyebrows. This was not going to be easy. After a pause, he curled his tongue toward the roof of his mouth and made the small sound of rolled r's that people use to call a cat.

The movement of Hathor's tail halted briefly and she turned toward the call.

Anhur stepped from the shadow and walked very slowly toward the huge cat, adding the noise of the sistrum to his summons.

Ra, alert to these new sounds, grew very still.

The lion's ears laid back.

Anhur ceased the sistrum for a moment and slipped the skin of beer off his shoulder. He unplugged it and flooded its dark, blood-colored contents on the ground before him.

The lion's ears turned forward again. She sniffed appreciatively and began to lap at the swirls of beer. Anhur began to walk gently toward her, swaying to the sound of the sistrum.

Right before his eyes, the paws of Hathor the Lion became hoofs. Her ears elongated. Her legs lengthened beneath her. Her pink tongue thickened. By the time Anhur reached her side, Hathor the Lion was Hathor the Cow once again. Only her tail had changed hardly at all, and she bellowed briefly, lifting her chin to be scratched.

Anhur scratched hard and fed her the nine cakes of barley, millet, and wheat. She munched contentedly, all trace of her irritation gone. Anhur slipped over Hathor's head the noose of the golden rope. Then he took one of Ra's hands.

And so it was that Anhur led Hathor the Cow and the Pharaoh Ra back from the land of Nubia. Up they climbed to the twelve kingdoms where all the gods and goddesses rejoiced. Shu the Air and Tefnut the Rain felt strength return to their limbs. Nut, tall, dark, and starry-eyed, stretched above them, as she does to this day, reaching out her fingers and toes to her husband, Geb, hairy green below her. Hathor the Cow took her place again as the Eye of Ra the Sun, who began to travel again west over the twelve kingdoms. By night he still sails peacefully through Mother Sky to be born again each morning. By day he reaches out his thousand glittering arms and hands, warming all he touches. Twice each day, Anhur carries to Hathor nine hundred pounds of fodder. He sweeps her bed a thousand strokes and washes it fresh and clean. Hathor, Eye of the Sun, lies like a queen, ruminating in all four of her stomachs about the ways of the world.

Mother Sun and the People

A PLAY

Characters:
Narrator
Mother Sun
Moon
Sun Daughter
The People (Chorus)
Little People (offstage voice)
Adder
Copperhead
Water Monster
Rattlesnake
Seven Men

Props:
masks, box facade, seven sticks, table, two chairs, bowls, spoons,
scarves for dancers to wave

PROLOGUE

NARRATOR: The Cherokee tell this story of a time when the earth got boiling hot, and then dark and freezing cold. At the beginning of our story, Mother Sun is not what she will become. She is petty and mean, unable to imagine the point of view of anyone but herself. High in the vault of the sky she lives, stopping at the house of Daughter Sun each noon for her lunch. Our play opens as Mother Sun takes up an old argument with Moon.

ACT I

In the sky vault.

MOON: Mother Sun, you are just too hot. Would you cool it a little?

MOTHER SUN: Oh, shut up, Moon. I'll shine just the way I please.

[The Moon *slumps, sighing loudly, shaking his head.*]

MOTHER SUN: Oh, stop it. You're always mooning around.

MOON: I can't help it. I feel sorry for them.

MOTHER SUN [*mimics*]: "I feel sorry for them." Yeah, well, you can afford to. They're always staring at you with those lovey-dovey faces—all soft and smiling. I'm sick of it! Just sick of it!

MOON: What, Mother Sun? What are you sick of?

MOTHER SUN: I'm sick of the way my grandchildren look at me. They squint up their faces every single time they turn their eyes on my face. They are ugly—every one of them.

But for you! Oh no! All you get, Moon, is smiles, smiles, smiles. I am sick of it.

MOON: I'm a gentle, mellow guy, Mother Sun. If you would lighten up, they'd probably love you, too. They are your grandkids. You should go easier on them.

MOTHER SUN: Humph! I'll do nothing of the sort! Easy, my rays! Never!

ACT II

At Sun Daughter's *house.*

SUN DAUGHTER: Hi Mom! Good to see you. [*She kisses her on both cheeks.*]

MOTHER SUN [*grumpily*]: You see me every day at lunchtime. What's the big deal?

SUN DAUGHTER: Whoa! Are we grumpy today, or what? What's the matter? [*She pulls out chair for mother. They begin to eat.*]

MOTHER SUN: The grandchildren. I've had it with them. Every one of them is ugly, and they show no respect whatsoever. I'm going to kill them.

SUN DAUGHTER: Mom, just calm down. You get so uptight. Here, have some of your favorite yellow squash soup. [*serves bowls*]

MOTHER SUN [*starting to sit down, but much too impatient*]: Humph! [*She goes outside and moves arms so that her blistering heat pours down to earth, shouting down*] I hope every last one of you gets fried to a crisp!

Act III

On earth.

CHORUS [*moaning and falling over, dying, ad-libbing*]: Ooooo!
We're dying! The Sun is too hot! We can't stand it. We're
boiling! We have fevers! Ooooooo! It's a plague, it's a
plague!
We've got to do something. There must be someway to stop
Mother Sun from this terrible crime she's committing
against us!
We'd better talk to the Little People.
Little People! Little People! Come with your friendly, powerful
medicine! We need you! We need you!

LITTLE PEOPLE [*offstage spooky voice*]: Mother Sun is trying to
kill you! There's only one thing to do. You have to kill her.

CHORUS [*looking at one another*]: We've got to kill her!! But
how, Little People, but how?

LITTLE PEOPLE: We've got the medicine to make snakes. They'll
do it: Here's Adder and Copperhead at your service!

[Adder *and* Copperhead *enter and take a bow.*]

CHORUS [*ad-lib while* Adder *and* Copperhead *strut around*]:
Give me an A. A! Give me a D. D! Give me a D. D! Give
me an E. E! Give me an R. R! What's that spell? ADDER!
[*and so on*] Go for it, you two! You can do it? Kill 'er!

Act IV

Outside Sun Daughter's *house.*
Adder and *Copperhead* slither up and wait for *Mother Sun* to arrive
for lunch.

COPPERHEAD: She should be here soon. She gets here at noon every day.

ADDER: Yeah! It shouldn't be long. It's 11:55.

COPPERHEAD: Boy, is she gonna be scared when she sees me. She'll probably die just from fright.

ADDER: Shhhhhhht! Here she comes!

[Mother Sun *walks proudly into view.* Adder *steps out in front of her.*]

ADDER: Aaaaaagh! [*covers eyes*] She's blinding me! [*Yellow slime comes out of his mouth.*]

MOTHER SUN [*taunting*]: Can't keep your dinner down, Little Worm? [*looks at* Copperhead, *who has begun to hiss*] You're just a nasty old thing. [*steps over him, and knocks on the door*] Honey! I'm here! Smells good! What'd you make today?

SUN DAUGHTER [*opening door*]: Hi, Mom. Come on in. We're having red pepper soup.

MOTHER SUN: Sounds great! You've got two scared little worms outside your door. Those brat grandchildren must have sent them. [*waves her arms*] Drop dead down there!

ACT V

On earth.

CHORUS: Oooooo! They failed! They failed! We're dying still. Help us!

LITTLE PEOPLE [*offstage spooky voice*]: Water Monster and Rattlesnake at your service. Trust us, these two have got what it takes.

[Water Monster *leaps out, gnashing his teeth.* Rattlesnake *follows with his rattle.*]

WATER MONSTER [*gnashing, roaring*]: After her! Death to the Sun!

RATTLESNAKE: Wait for me!

CHORUS: They can do it, they can do it! They can, they can!

ACT VI

In front of Sun Daughter's *house.*
Water Monster *and* Rattlesnake *come running onstage, panting.*

RATTLESNAKE: Where is she? Where is she?

WATER MONSTER: Slow down, Rattlesnake! This is a job for a big guy.

SUN DAUGHTER [*opening her door*]: Is that you, Mom?

RATTLESNAKE: That's her! Death!

[*He strikes* Sun Daughter, *who falls down, with a piercing cry, dead.*]

WATER MONSTER [*lunging after* Rattlesnake]: You little fool! That's the kid, not the mother. Idiot! Slimeball!

[*He hits* Rattlesnake, *who is whimpering, realizing his mistake.* Mother Sun *enters.*]

RATTLESNAKE: We better get outa here!

[Rattlesnake *and* Water Monster *back off stage.*]

MOTHER SUN [*with gut-wrenching scream*]: No! No! Not my baby! My beloved! My daughter! No, no, no, no, no. [*She takes* Sun Daughter's *body in her arms.*]

CHORUS [*offstage this time, makes thin ghostly music mixed with human crying*]: And so Sun Daughter's spirit rose up and joined the dead grandchildren in the Ghost Country . . . Ghost Country . . . Ghost Country. [*Human crying sound mixes with* Mother Sun's *crying.*]

ACT VII

On a completely dark earth (no lights, or candles only). Mother Sun *is cloaked in black and huddled on floor on stage.*

CHORUS [*in two simultaneous, increasingly anguished parts*]:

1. She won't come out. She won't come out. She won't come out. She won't come out. She won't come out. She won't come out.

2. Dark. Dark. Dark. Dark. Dark. Dark. Dark. Dark. Dark. Dark.

LITTLE PEOPLE [*offstage spooky voice*]: It's seven men with seven sticks with a good strong box who must bring her back. Bring back the ghost daughter. Bring her back. Bring her back.

CHORUS [*joining in*]: Bring her back! Bring her back! Bring her back! Bring her back!

LITTLE PEOPLE: But whatever you do . . .

CHORUS: Whatever you do . . .

LITTLE PEOPLE: Whatever you do, don't open that box . . .

CHORUS: Don't open that box.

LITTLE PEOPLE: No matter how much she begs, don't open that box . . .

CHORUS [*simultaneously in two parts*]:

1. Bring her back!

2. Don't open that box!

[*Continue chanting while seven men with seven sticks and a good strong box step from* Chorus *and "walk in place" to the Ghost Country.* Chorus *members put on ghost masks or cloaks and begin to move in circle to drum beat.* Sun Daughter *in ghost mask with red dress is part of chorus.*]

> CHORUS [*changing chant*]: We are the ghosts, ghosts, ghosts, ghosts, ghosts, ghosts, ghosts, of the ones that were. [*Repeat, while one member only chants:*] Bring her back, don't open that box.

[*The* Seven Men *touch* Sun Daughter *with sticks, lower the box over her, and "walk in place" in opposite direction.* Chorus *takes off ghost masks, moves rhythmically behind* Seven Men *as chant continues:*]

> Bring her back, don't open that box!
>
> SUN DAUGHTER [*from inside box*]: Pleeeaaase! Let me out!
>
> SEVEN MEN: We can't. We're not supposed to. We can't. We're not supposed to.

[Chorus *silences.*]

> SUN DAUGHTER [*pitiously*]: I'm hungry! Let me out!
>
> SEVEN MEN [*stop moving*]: We can't. They said not to. Just wait. Please wait.
>
> SUN DAUGHTER [*wailing*]: I'm suffocating! I can't breathe. I'm going to die.
>
> SEVEN MEN: Just a crack. We'll bring her back. Just a crack can't hurt. She's dying!

[*They open the box, and* Sun Daughter *springs out in the form of* Redbird.]

SEVEN MEN: What was that?

CHORUS [*to tune of "Here we go 'round the mulberry bush"*]: Redbird is the Sun Daughter, the Sun Daughter, the Sun Daughter. Redbird is the Sun Daughter for ever and a day.

[*The song repeats while one member intones:*] The men opened the box and Sun Daughter got away. Forever after, no one has been able to bring anyone else back from the Ghost Country. It was just a crack, but there's no going back. They opened the box.

MOTHER SUN [*rising partially from floor, still cloaked in black, emitting gigantic wail*]: Never, never, never, never, never!

CHORUS [*half*]: She won't come out! Dark, dark, dark. She won't come out!

MOTHER SUN [*simultaneous*]: Never, never, never.

CHORUS [*half*]: We must send the young people! The young people can dance and sing for her.

[*Drum beats begin;* Chorus *members take out scarves.*]

CHORUS [*half*]: [*slowly*] Beat the drums, move the feet, sing the song. [*Repeat several times.*]

CHORUS [*half*]: Send the young people. [*Repeat several times.*]

LITTLE PEOPLE [*offstage*]: Send the young people.

SUN DAUGHTER [*as bird*]: Send the young people.

[*The* Chorus *dances slowly around and around* Mother Sun, *who is silent, head bowed in center, shoulders shaking, paying no attention to dancers.*]

CHORUS [*sadly, heads bowed, and beautifully*]: Mourning, mourning, mourning, mourning, mourning . . . [*Drum beats suddenly shift to much faster tempo. Heads of chorus members lift.*] Morning! Morning! Morning! Morning!

MOTHER SUN [*stiffens, as if hearing for first time. Lifts head. Peaks through her fingers. Looks harder*]: It's my grand-children. [*sits up straight*] It's my grandchildren.

CHORUS [*continues*]: Morning! Morning! Morning! Morning!

MOTHER SUN: They're alive. [*stands up*] They're not ugly at all. They're beautiful.

[*She spreads her arms. Lights flood stage.*]

[*Dancing breaks loose with cheering, everyone on stage, with Mother Sun beaming at center.*]

Bibliography

Abraham, Ralph, Terence McKenna, and Rupert Sheldrake. *Trialogues at the Edge of the West: Chaos, Creativity, and the Resacralization of the World*. Santa Fe: Bear & Co., 1992.

Belting, Natalia. *The Long-Tailed Bear and Other Indian Legends*. New York: Bobbs-Merrill Co., 1961.

Bernstein, Burton. *Sinai: The Great and Terrible Wilderness*. New York: Viking Press, 1979.

Bernstein, Margery, and Janet Kobrin. *The First Morning: An African Myth*. New York: Charles Scribner's Sons, 1972.

Bierhorst, John, trans. *Cantares Mexicanos: Songs of the Aztecs: Translated from the Nahuatl with an Introduction and Commentary*. Stanford: Stanford Univ. Press, 1985.

Bonnefoy, Yves, and Wendy Doniger, ed. *Mythologies: A Restructured Translation of Dictionnaire des mythologies et des religions des sociétés traditionnelles et du monde antique*. Chicago: Univ. of Chicago Press, 1991.

Bratton, Fred Gladstone. *The First Heretic: The Life and Times of Ikhnaton the King*. Boston: Beacon Press, 1961.

Burland, C. A. *The Gods of Mexico*. New York: G. P. Putnam's Sons, 1967.

Burns, Marilyn. *The Hanukkah Book*. New York: Four Winds Press, 1981.

Campbell, Joseph. *The Flight of the Wild Gander: Explorations in Mythological Dimensions of Fairy Tales, Legends, and Symbols*. New York: Harper Perennial, 1951.

Carpenter, Frances. *The Elephant's Bathtub: Wonder Tales from the Far East*. New York: Doubleday & Co., 1962.

Cassier, Ernst. *Language and Myth*. New York: Dover Publications, 1953.

Catholic University of America. *New Catholic Encyclopedia*. Vol. 1. New York: McGraw Hill, 1979.

Cavendish, Richard, ed. *Man, Myth, and Magic: The Illustrated Encyclopedia of Mythology, Religion, and the Unknown*. New York: Marshall Cavendish, 1983.

————. *Mythology: An Illustrated Encyclopedia*. New York: Rizzoli International Publications, 1980.

Cathon, Laura, and Thusnelda Schmidt. *Perhaps and Perchance: Tales of Nature*. New York: Abingdon Press, 1962.

Clark, Ronald W. *Edison: The Man Who Made the Future*. New York: G. P. Putnam's Sons, 1977.

Cosner, Sharon. *The Light Bulb*. New York: Walker, 1984.

Cothran, Jean, ed. *The Magic Calabash: Folk Tales from America's Islands and Alaska*. New York: David McKay Co., 1956.

Courlander, Harold. *The Tiger's Whisker and Other Tales and Legends from Asia and the Pacific.* New York: Harcourt, Brace & Co., 1959.

Covarrubias, Miguel. *The Eagle, the Jaguar, and the Serpent: Indian Art of the Americas.* New York: Alfred A. Knopf, 1954.

Cunningham, Caroline. *The Talking Stone: being Early American Stories told before the white man's day on this continent by the Indians and Eskimos.* New York: Alfred A. Knopf, 1939.

Curry, Jane Louise. *Down from the Lonely Mountain: California Indian Tales.* New York: Harcourt, Brace & World, 1965.

Davies, Nigel. *The Toltecs: Until the Fall of Tula.* Norman: Univ. of Oklahoma Press, 1977.

Davis, Russell, and Brent Ashabranner. *Ten Thousand Desert Swords.* Boston: Little, Brown & Co., 1960.

Drucker, Malka. *Hanukkah: Eight Nights, Eight Lights.* New York: Holiday House, 1980.

Edgerton, Robert B. *Mau Mau: An African Crucible.* New York: Free Press, 1989.

Edwards, Carolyn McVickar. *The Storyteller's Goddess.* San Francisco: HarperSanFrancisco, 1991.

Eliade, Mircea, ed. *Encyclopedia of Religion.* New York: Macmillan, 1987.

Elwin, Verrier. *Tribal Myths of the Orissa.* New York: Oxford Univ. Press, 1954.

Estés, Clarissa Pinkola. *Women Who Run with the Wolves.* New York: Ballantine, 1992.

Fideler, David. *Jesus Christ, Sun of God: Ancient Cosmology and Early Christian Symbolism.* Wheaton, IL: Quest Books, 1993.

Fitzgerald, C. P. *China: A Short Cultural History*. New York: Praeger Publishers, 1972.

Gastor, H. Theodor. *The Oldest Stories in the World*. Boston: Beacon Press, 1952.

Gimbutas, Marija. *The Balts*. New York: Frederick A. Praeger, 1963.

Gleik, James. *Chaos: Making a New Science*. New York: Penguin, 1987.

Grahn, Judy. *Blood, Bread and Roses: How Menstruation Created the World*. Boston: Beacon Press, 1993.

Gray, John. *Near Eastern Mythology: Mesopotamia, Syria, Palestine*. New York: Hamlyn Publishing Group, 1969.

Greenberg, Judith, and Helen H. Carey. *Jewish Holidays: A First Book*. New York: Franklin Watts, 1984.

Gregory, Horace, and Marya Zaturenska. *The Silver Swan: Poems of Romance and Mystery*. New York: Holt, Rinehart & Winston, 1966.

Griffith, Ralph T. H. *Hymns of the Atharrveda*. Vol. 2. New Delhi: Munshiram Manoharlal Publishers, 1985.

Grimal, Pierre, ed. *Laurousse World Mythology*. New York: G. P. Putnam's Sons, 1963.

Grousset, René. *The Rise and Splendor of the Chinese Empire*. Berkeley: Univ. of California Press, 1953.

Hamilton, Edith. *Mythology: Timeless Tales of Gods and Heroes*. Boston: Little, Brown & Co., 1942.

Haviland, Virginia, ed. *North American Legends*. New York: Collins, 1979.

Hedges, Lawrence. *Interpreting Countertransference*. Northvale, NJ: Jason Aronson, 1992.

Helfman, Elizabeth. *The Bushmen and Their Stories*. New York: Seabury Press, 1971.

Hobley, C. W. *Bantu Beliefs and Magic, with particular reference to Kikuyu and Kamba tribes of Kenya Colony; together with some reflections on East Africa after the war.* 1922. Reprint, New York: Barnes & Noble, 1967.

Hooke, Samuel Henry. *Middle Eastern Mythology: From the Assyrians to the Hebrews*. New York: Penguin, 1963.

Hume, Lotta Carswell. *Favorite Children's Stories from China and Tibet*. Rutland, VT: Charles E. Tuttle Co., 1962.

Hyde, Lewis. *The Gift: Imagination and the Erotic Life of Property*. New York: Vintage Books, 1979.

Johnsgard, Paul A. *The Hummingbirds of North America*. Washington, DC: Smithsonian Institution Press, 1983.

Johnson, Sandy and Dan Budnick. *The Book of Elders*. San Francisco: HarperSanFrancisco, 1994.

Jung, Carl G. *Modern Man in Search of a Soul*. New York: Harcourt, Brace & World, 1933.

————. Violet S. Laszlo, ed. *Psyche and Symbol*. New York: Anchor Books, 1958.

————. *Psychology and Religion*. New Haven, CT: Yale Univ. Press, 1938.

Kaplan, Irving. *Tanzania: A Country Study*. Washington, DC: American Univ. Press, 1978.

Kraft, John. *The Goddess in the Labyrinth*. Åbo, Sweden: Akaemi, 1985.

Langlois, John D., ed. *China Under Mongol Rule*. Princeton: Princeton Univ. Press, 1981.

León-Portilla, Miguel. *Pre-Columbian Literatures of Mexico*. Norman: Univ. of Oklahoma Press, 1969.

Levene, Ricardo. *A History of Argentina*. Chapel Hill: Univ. of North Carolina Press, 1937.

McCrickard, Janet. *Eclipse of the Sun: An Investigation into Sun and Moon Myths*. Glastonbury, Somerset: Gothic Image Publications, 1990.

McDowell, Robert E., and Edward Lavitt. *Third World Voices for Children*. New York: Odakai Books, 1971.

Manning-Sanders, Ruth. *A Book of Charms and Changelings*. New York: E. P. Dutton & Co., 1971.

Markman, Roberta H., and Peter T. Markman. *The Flayed God: The Mythology of Mesoamerica: Sacred Texts and Images from Pre-Columbian Mexico and Central America*. San Francisco: HarperSanFrancisco, 1992.

Martin, Fran. *Nine Tales of Coyote*. New York: Harper & Brothers, 1950.

Matson, Emerson N. *Legends of the Great Chiefs*. Nashville, TN: Thomas Nelson, 1972.

May, Rollo. *The Cry for Myth*. New York: W. W. Norton & Co., 1991.

Mayhall, Mildred P. *The Kiowas*. Norman: Univ. of Oklahoma Press. 1962.

Melzack, Ronald. *The Day Tuk Became a Hunter and Other Eskimo Stories*. New York: Dodd, Mead & Co., 1967.

———. *Raven: Creator of the World*. Boston: Little, Brown & Co., 1970.

Miles, Clement A. *Christmas Customs and Traditions: Their History and Significance*. New York: Dover Publications, 1976.

Mindell, Arnold. *The Leader as Martial Artist: An Introduction to Deep Democracy: Techniques and Strategies for Resolving Conflict and Creating Community*. San Francisco: HarperSanFrancisco, 1993.

———. *Working with the Dreaming Body*. London: Routledge & Kegan Paul, 1985.

———. *Working on Yourself Alone: Inner Dreambody Work*. New York: Arkana Penguin, 1990.

Moore, Thomas. *Soul Mates: Honoring the Mysteries of Love and Relationship*. New York: HarperCollins, 1994.

Müller, F. Max. *The Sacred Books of the East*. Vol. 42. Oxford: Clarendon Press, 1897.

Muñoz de Coronado, Martha. *Como Sugieron Los Seres y Las Cosas*. Lima, Peru: Coedición Latinoamericana, 1986.

Olson, Carl, ed. *The Book of the Goddess Past and Present: An Introduction to Her Religion*. New York: Crossroad, 1992.

Nicholson, Irene. *Mexican and Central American Mythology*. New York: Peter Bedrich Books, 1985.

O'Flaherty, Wendy Doniger. *Women, Androgynes, and Other Mythical Beasts*. Chicago: Univ. of Chicago Press, 1980.

Parrinder, Geoffrey. *African Mythology*. London: Paul Hamlyn, 1967.

Peck, M. Scott. *The Different Drum: Community Making and Peace: A Spiritual Journey Toward Self-Acceptance, True Belonging, and New Hope for the World*. New York: Simon & Schuster, 1987.

————. *The Road Less Traveled: A New Psychology of Love, Traditional Values and Spiritual Growth*. New York: Simon & Schuster, 1978.

Peters, F. E. *Allah's Commonwealth: A History of Islam in the Near East 600–1100 A.D.* New York: Simon & Schuster, 1973.

Peterson, Roger Tory. *Western Birds*. Boston: Houghton Mifflin Co., 1990.

Ponting, Clive. *A Green History of the World: The Environment and the Collapse of Great Civilizations*. New York: St. Martin's Press, 1991.

Prabhavananda, Swami, and Frederick Manchester, trans. *The Upanishads: Breath of the Eternal*. Hollywood: Vedanta Society of Southern California, 1957.

Radin, Paul. *The Trickster: A Study in American Indian Mythology*. New York: Schocken Books, 1972.

Rasmussen, Knud. *Eskimo Songs and Stories*. New York: Delacorte Press, 1973.

Rennie, Ysabel F. *The Argentine Republic*. New York: Macmillan, 1945.

Reuben, Joel. *Kenya . . . in Pictures*. Minneapolis: Lerner Publications, 1991.

Rifkin, Jeremy. *Entropy: A New World View*. New York: Viking Press, 1980.

Robinson, Gail, and Douglas Hill. *Coyote the Trickster: Legends of the North American Indians*. New York: Crane & Russack, 1975.

Robinson, James M., ed. *The Nag Hammadi Library*. San Francisco: Harper & Row, 1988.

Rosenblum, William F., and Robert J. Rosenblum. *Eight Lights: The Story of Chanukah*. Garden City, NY: Doubleday & Co., 1967.

Rossi, Ernest Laurence. *The Twenty Minute Break: Using the New Science of Ultradian Rhythms*. Los Angeles: Jeremy P. Tarcher, 1991.

Rushdie, Salman. *The Satanic Verses*. New York: Viking, 1988.

Scobie, James R. *Argentina: A City and a Nation*. New York: Oxford Univ. Press, 1964.

Seed, Jenny. *The Bushman's Dream: African Tales of the Creation*. Scarsdale, NY: Bradbury Press, 1974.

Shah, Indries. *The Sufis*. Garden City, NY: Doubleday & Co., 1964.

Sheldrake, Rupert. *The Rebirth of Nature: The Greening of Science and God*. New York: Bantam Books, 1991.

Skinner, Fred Gladstone. *Myths and Legends of the Ancient Near East*. New York: Barnes & Noble, 1970.

Skutch, Alexander. *The Life of the Hummingbird*. New York: Crown Publishers, 1973.

Singer, June. *Seeing Through the Visible World: Jung, Gnosis, and Chaos*. San Francisco: HarperSanFrancisco, 1990.

Small, Arnold. *The Birds of California*. New York: Winchester Press, 1974.

Sullivan, Laurence E. *Icanchu's Drum: An Orientation to Meaning in South American Religions*. New York: Macmillan, 1988.

Swan, Michael. *The Marches of El Dorado: British Guiana, Brazil, Venezuela*. London: Jonathan Cape, 1958.

Thompson, Vivian L. *Maui-Full-Of-Tricks*. San Carlos, CA: Golden Gate Junior Books, 1970.

Tompkins, Ptolemy. *This Tree Grows Out of Hell: The Mesoamerican Search for the Magical Body*. San Francisco: HarperSanFrancisco, 1990.

Weatherford, J. McIver. *Indian Givers: How the Indians of the Americas Transformed the World*. New York: Crown, 1988.

———. *Native Roots: How the Indians Enriched America*. New York: Crown, 1991.

Wherry, Joseph H. *Indian Masks and Myths of the West*. New York: Bonanza Books, 1969.

Whitaker, Arthur P. *Argentina*. Englewood Cliffs, NJ: Prentice Hall, 1964.

Wilcock, John. *Traveling in Venezuela*. New York: Hippocrene Books, 1979.

Wilson, H. H. *The Vishnu Purana: A System of Hindu Mythology and Tradition*. Calcutta: Punthi Pustak, 1972.

Wunder, John R. *The Kiowa*. New York: Chelsea House Publishers, 1989.

Story and Motif Index

Each story is identified in this index by the name of its people of origin.

Stories

Balts: "The Sun, the Stars, the Tower, and the Hammer," 108.
Canaan: "How Shapash the Sun Rescued the Prince of Fertility," 13.
Cherokee: "Mother Sun and Her People," 5.
Christian: "The Christmas Story," 128.
Egypt: "Ra and Hathor," 169.
Greece: "Baubo's Dance," 36.
Haida: "Seagull's Box," 148.
Hindu: "Surya the Sun's Marriage to Bright and Shadow," 51.
Inuit: "Raven and the Theft of Light," 139.
Italy: "The Story of La Befana," 134.
Jewish: "The Chanukah Story," 120.
Kiowa: "Spider Grandmother Finds Light for Her People," 24.
Kuttia Kond: "The Sun Cow and the Thief," 83.

Luhya: "The Rope from Heaven," 61.

Miwok: "How Marsh Wren Shot Out the Sun," 88.

Miao-tzu: "How the Cock Got His Crown," 73.

Polynesia: "Maui Snares the Sun," 152.

San: "Sun Man and Grandfather Mantis," 103.

Slavs: "Solntse, the Girl at the End of the World," 117.

Snohomish: "How the Sun Came to Belong to Every Village," 66.

Sukuma: "Harambee: The Story of the Pull-Together Morning," 29.

Thai: "The Marriage of Sun King and Silver Moon," 92.

Thoria: "Sonwari and the Golden Earring," 78.

Toba:" Web of Fear: The Story of Akewa the Sun and Jaguar Man,"
43.

Toltec: "Fifth Sun," 160.

Warao: "The Light Keeper's Box," 98.

Motifs

aloneness: Balts, 108; Cherokee, 5; Greece, 36; Hindu, 51; Italy, 134;
Kiowa, 24; Kuttia Kond, 83; Luhya, 61; Miwok, 88; Slavs, 117;
Snohomish, 66; Thoria, 78; Toba, 43

animism: Kuttia Kond, 83; Miwok, 88; Miao-tzu, 73; San, 103; Thoria, 78; Warao, 98. See also polytheism.

angel: Christian, 128

animals, as main characters: Egypt, 169; Haida, 148; Inuit, 139;
Kiowa, 24; Kuttia Kond, 83; Miwok, 88; San, 103; Sukuma, 29;
Toba, 43. See also bird, cow, mouse, spider, trickster.

animals, figuring in story: Balts, 108; Cherokee, 5; Christian, 128;
Greece, 36; Hindu, 51; Italy, 134; Miao-tzu, 73; Polynesia, 152;
Snohomish, 66; Thai, 92; Warao, 98. See also horses, trickster.

arrows: Miwok, 88; Miao-tzu, 73; Snohomish, 66

bird: Cherokee (redbird), 5; Christian (rooster), 128; Egypt (falcon),
169; Greece (miscellaneous), 36; Haida (raven, seagull), 148;

Inuit (raven), 139; Kiowa (eagle, woodpecker), 24; Miwok (marsh wren, hummingbird), 88; Miao-tzu (rooster), 73; Polynesia, 152; San (blue heron), 103; Sukuma (rooster), 29; Thoria (kite), 78; Toba (falcon), 43; Toltec, 160

blacksmith. *See* smith.

birth: Christian, 128; Egypt, 169; Hindu, 51; Thai, 92; Toltec, 160

box: Cherokee, 5; Haida, 148; Sukuma, 29; Thoria, 78; Warao, 98. *See also* container.

child, children: Canaan , 13; Cherokee, 5; Christian, 128; Egypt, 169; Greece, 36; Hindu, 51; Inuit, 139; Italy, 134; Luhya, 61; Miwok, 88; Polynesia, 152; San, 103; Slavs, 117; Snohomish, 66; Thai, 92; Warao, 98

Chanukah: Jewish, 120

Christmas: Christian, 128; Italy, 134

cock: Miao-tzu, 73; Sukuma, 29

community: Balts, 108; Canaan, 13; Cherokee, 5; Egypt, 169; Greece, 36; Hindu, 51; Jewish, 120; Kiowa, 24; Kuttia Kond, 83; Miwok, 88; Miao-tzu, 73; Polynesia, 152; Snohomish, 66; Sukuma, 29; Toltec, 160; Warao, 98

container: Inuit, 139; Italy, 134; Kiowa, 24; Luhya, 61. *See also* box.

contest: Canaan, 13; Cherokee, 5; Kiowa, 24; Miao-tzu, 73; Polynesia, 152; Sukuma, 29; Snohomish, 66; Toltec, 160

couple: Canaan, 13; Christain, 128; Egypt, 169; Hindu, 51; Inuit, 139; Jewish, 120; Luhya, 61; San, 103; Snohomish, 66; Thai, 92; Thoria, 78; Toba, 43; Warao, 98

cow: Christian, 128; Egypt, 169; Hindu, 51; Kuttia Kond, 83; Luhya, 61; Miao-tzu, 73; Thoria, 78

dance: Cherokee, 5; Greece, 36

daughter. *See* child.

friendship: Sukuma, 29; Thoria, 78; Warao, 98

genders, struggle of, contrast of: Egypt, 169; Hindu, 51; Kiowa, 24; San, 103; Snohomish, 66; Thoria, 78; Toba, 43. *See also* couple.

gift: Canaan, 13; Christian, 128; Italy, 134; Luhya, 61; Warao, 98. *See also* sacrifice.

grief: Balts, 108; Canaan, 13; Cherokee, 5; Christian, 128; Egypt,
    169; Greece, 36; Inuit, 139; Jewish, 120; Kuttia Kond, 83;
    Miwok, 88; Snohomish, 66; Thoria, 78; Toba, 43; Toltec, 160
hammer: Balts, 108; Jewish, 120. *See also* smith.
Hannukah. *See* Chanukah.
horses: Balts, 108; Greece, 36; Hindu, 51; Thai, 92
Jesus: Christian, 128; Italy, 134; Toltec, 160
Kwanza: Sukuma, 29. *See also* community.
light. *See* sun.
loneliness. *See* aloneness.
loss. *See* grief.
monotheism: Christian, 128; Egypt, 169; Italy, 134; Jewish, 120
mother: Cherokee, 5; Christian, 128; Egypt, 169; Greece, 36; Hindu,
    51; Inuit, 139; Luhya, 61; Polynesia, 152; Slavs, 117; Sno-
    homish, 66; Thoria, 78; Toltec, 160
mourning. *See* grief.
mouse: Snohomish, 66; Sukuma, 29
old man: Canaan, 13; Egypt, 169; Hindu, 51; Inuit, 139; Jewish,
    120; San, 103; Snohomish, 66; Thoria, 78; Warao, 98
old woman: Cherokee, 5; Greece, 36; Italy, 134; Kiowa, 24; Luhya,
    61; Polynesia, 152; San, 103; Slavs, 117
polytheism: Balts, 108; Canaan, 13; Cherokee, 5; Egypt, 169; Greece,
    36; Hindu, 51; Inuit, 139; Kiowa, 24; Luhya, 61; Polynesia,
    152; Slavs, 117; Snohomish, 66; Sukuma, 29; Thai, 92; Toba,
    43; Toltec, 160. *See also* animism.
red, color: Balts, 108; Canaan, 13; Cherokee, 5; Christian, 128;
    Egypt, 169; Hindu, 51; Italy, 134; Luhya, 61; Miwok, 88;
    Miao-tzu, 169; Slavs, 117; Sukuma, 29
rope: Egypt, 169; Kiowa (thread), 24; Luhya, 61; Polynesia, 152;
    Toba, 43
rooster. *See* cock.
sacrifice: Cherokee, 5; Christian, 128; Jewish, 120; Luhya, 61; Sno-
    homish, 66; Toltec, 160. *See also* gift.
smith, heavenly: Balts, 108; Canaan, 13; Hindu, 51

son. *See* child.

spider: Kiowa, 24; Sukuma, 29

stars: Balts, 108; Christian, 128; Inuit, 139; San, 103; Thai, 92

sun, birth of: Christian, 128; Egypt, 169; Hindu, 51; Italy, 134; Thoria, 78; Toltec, 160

sun, female: Balts, 108; Canaan, 13; Cherokee, 5; Egypt, 169; Hindu, 51; Kuttia Kond, 83; Miwok (see introduction), 88; Slavs, 117; Toba, 43

sun (or light) hiding, needing retrieval: Balts, 108; Cherokee, 5; Egypt , 169; Greece, 36; Haida, 148; Inuit, 139; Jewish, 120; Kuttia Kond, 83; Luhya, 61; Miwok, 88; Miao-tzu, 73; Snohomish, 66; Thai, 92

sun, male: Christian, 128; Egypt, 169; Greece, 36; Hindu, 51; Luhya, 61; Polynesia, 152; San, 103; Thai, 92; Toltec, 160

sun, (or light) as object: Haida, 148; Inuit, 139; Jewish, 120; Kiowa, 24; Miwok, 88; Snohomish, 66; Sukuma, 29; Thoria, 78; Warao, 98

sun, personified. *See* sun, female; sun, male.

sun (or light) retrieved, returns. *See* sun, hiding; sun, sleeping.

sun, sleeping: San, 103; Slavs, 117

theft: Haida, 148; Inuit, 139; Kiowa, 24; Kuttia Kond, 83; Sukuma, 29; Thai, 92; Thoria, 78; Toba, 43

trick: Cherokee, 5; Egypt, 169; Haida, 148; Hindu, 51; Inuit, 139; Miao-tzu , 73; Polynesia, 152; Sukuma, 29; Thai, 92; Toba, 43

trickster: Egypt (Anhur), 169; Haida (Raven), 148; Inuit (Raven), 139; Miwok (Coyote), 88; Polynesia (Maui), 152; San (Mantis), 103

underworld: Canaan, 13; Cherokee, 5; Egypt, 169; Greece, 36

war: Canaan, 13; Hindu (weapons), 51; Jewish, 120

web, appearance of by stars or sun rays: Christian, 128; Polynesia, 152; Thoria, 78. *See also* rope, spider.

zodiac: Balts, 108. *See also* stars.